Death at the Craven Arms

Veronica Vale Investigates - book 3

Kitty Kildare

K.E. O'Connor Books

Copyright © 2024 by Kitty Kildare

All rights reserved.

No part of this publication may be reproduced, distributed, or transmitted in any form or by any means, including photocopying, recording, or other electronic or mechanical methods, without the prior written permission of the publisher, except as permitted by U.S. copyright law. For permission requests, contact: kittykildare@kittykildare.com

The story, all names, characters, and incidents portrayed in this production are fictitious. No identification with actual persons (living or deceased), places, buildings, and products is intended or should be inferred.

DEATH AT THE CRAVEN ARMS

ISBN: 978-1-915378-79-8

Book Cover by Victoria Cooper

Chapter 1

"I knew this would be the perfect venue to see a ghost," a plump middle-aged woman wearing a red cloche hat over her dark curls exclaimed, as her friend sat beside her. "Look how old everything is! The beams are crumbling. And that fireplace is divine."

"I read the Craven Arms has six ghosts!" her companion said. "And all murdered on the premises. How gruesome."

They tittered together, their heads bent close as they continued their discussion so they could hear each other over the mumble of other conversations.

I held in a less than respectable snort and took a large, fortifying sip from my delicious gin fizz. I'd need something stronger than this to prepare myself if the night continued in this fashion. I looked around the surprisingly crowded interior of the low-ceilinged pub. Who'd have thought searching for spirits would be so popular and profitable? When I'd agreed, somewhat reluctantly, to permit the Craven Arms to be hired for a night of ghost hunting and a reading from a ghost hunter's journal, I hadn't expected the tickets to sell out. There was even a queue of hopefuls outside in the dingy gloom, eager to procure a last-minute cancellation so they could be in the presence of William Lombard, self-proclaimed ghost hunter extraordinaire, and to my mind, an absolute fraud.

"Need a top-up, Veronica?" Joe Patterson, my able-bodied and reliable publican, slid a fresh gin fizz towards me. "From the look on your face, you need it."

"Is my disbelief so terribly obvious?" I gratefully accepted the drink.

"We shouldn't complain. The ghosts are great for business." He chortled at my displeasure before striding along behind the bar to serve several waiting customers, all eager to see a different kind of spirit in their glasses. "No Ruby?"

"Late, as usual," I replied.

"Got herself a new man?"

"No. A difficult employer."

Joe chortled again. "I know the feeling."

"Is that William?" The woman in the cloche hat grabbed her friend's arm. "I recognise that profile. He has a handsome Roman nose."

Her friend sighed. "No, that's not him. Mr Lombard is a genius. We're so fortunate he came all this way."

"He must sense a strong presence in these walls."

"Some people have a natural connection to ghosts. They see through to the other side and call them back to us."

"What nonsense," I muttered, gently patting Benji on the head. My ever-loyal dog had tucked himself behind my bar stool to avoid getting his tail trodden on by overexcited ghost hunters.

I lifted a copy of the book I'd snuck off Mr Lombard's sales table. I turned it over and inspected his author photograph. Dark hair and eyes. Expensive suit. He insincerely smiled at me, no doubt delighted with himself for fleecing so many innocent types of their hard-earned money. His biography listed him as an expert in the field of the paranormal, with an innate ability to uncover the secrets of the dead. This was his third published book, and this edition contained journal accounts of twenty pubs and taverns he'd investigated for alleged paranormal behaviour.

Unbeknownst to me, Mr Lombard had spent three days at the Craven Arms conducting an unofficial investigation. If I'd known what he'd been up to, I'd never have permitted it. The Craven Arms was one of my family's concerns, and I'd have insisted this nonsense be stopped. Ghosts weren't real.

Well, I didn't believe in them. My mother had briefly had an interest in the afterlife. She'd even been involved with a spiritualist church in Hackney.

"I suppose you'll get that signed when the chap shows his face." Joe returned with a tray of freshly washed glasses.

"I'm no more a ghost hunter than I am an autograph hunter," I said. "All this twittering and flapping. Anyone would think Humphrey Bogart was about to perform. I'm astonished so many people have turned out to hear this paranormal claptrap."

"It's not the reading they're excited about." Joe unloaded the glasses onto empty shelves behind the well-worn bar. "They're all hoping to see a ghost. Are you staying for the investigation? There's food laid on, too."

"What else would I do on such a ghastly night? It's perfect weather to invite the spirits in." It was a dreary, foggy evening. My mother had almost had apoplexy when I'd told her I would be out late investigating ghosts. She'd insisted I wrap myself in three scarves before leaving the house.

There was a thump, followed by several feminine shrieks. A pile of the author's books had slid off the table and fallen to the floor. Most likely knocked over by a passing customer.

"The ghosts are making their presence felt." Joe chuckled loudly, enjoying all the highly strung shenanigans.

I walked over and dealt with the messy pile, sorting it into a neat order so it wouldn't get knocked again, then returned to the bar and Benji.

"Which of our ghosts do you think played that prank?" Joe asked. "We've got our grey lady. She's often seen drifting around the outdoor toilet if you believe the gentlemen who visit. And then there's our headless horseman."

I speared him with an acerbic glare. "We do not have a headless horseman."

"Why not? He's as real as the grey lady. What about the ghostly crying you hear just after the stroke of midnight? Gets the hairs on the back of your neck tingling. And then we have—"

"You're only encouraging people to think foolish things by taking part in this fiction," I said.

"Is that what you'll say in your article?" Joe asked.

I had yet to withdraw my notepad from my handbag. I wouldn't have bothered attending this evening's charade, but I'd promised Uncle Harry I'd write an article for the London Times. None of the other journalists were interested in the story, and since my family's name was on the pub license, it seemed right I undertook this thankless task.

"I shall write the truth. Tell people exactly what I see."

"Or what you don't see," Joe said. "Don't be too harsh. Our trade booms after an investigation."

I lowered my glass. "This is the first I'm hearing about any paranormal tosh going on here."

"Your old dad was always up for it. In my time here, he hosted half a dozen paranormal events. We got all kinds of oddballs here with strange devices, listening for ghosts, and testing the water."

My eyes widened. "Testing the water for what?"

Joe laughed at my startled expression. "That one had me stumped, too. Be back in a moment." He dashed away to serve more thirsty customers.

"Miss Vale, I hope you're looking forward to this evening."

I turned and shook hands with Nicholas Hawthorn. We were business acquaintances, and I'd been dealing with him in his capacity as Mr Lombard's publisher. When he'd contacted me to suggest the event, I'd turned him down. But his offer grew so large, I'd found it impossible to refuse. I didn't want the money to line my pockets, but there was work needed at the dogs' home I volunteered at, so the fee was going there.

"Good evening, Mr Hawthorn."

"Please, call me Nicholas. We have an excellent attendance." He spoke with an over-the-top posh accent of someone attempting to reside in a class he wasn't born into.

"I'm surprised by the number of women here," I said.

"My client is known as something of a charmer," Nicholas said. "A ladies' man."

"What does his wife think about that?"

"William is married to his work. And besides, why settle for one lady when you can have all of these?" Nicholas gestured at the room. There were almost a hundred people waiting for Mr Lombard to arrive, and nearly all of them were ladies. Most were older than me, although there were a few younger ones in the crowd. I even spotted one or two grumpy husbands, who'd either been dragged here by their wives or had ventured out to ensure Mr Lombard wasn't too much of a charlatan.

"I fear your crowd will be disappointed," I said. "The Craven Arms has no ghosts. I spent many years here when I was younger. It was one of my father's favourite pubs."

"Your father is no longer with us? I was surprised to discover you were in charge of operations."

"He's been gone for some time. And it's a family concern. We all pitch in."

"Perhaps you'll see him tonight. William has a way of finding the spirits."

I thumped the book I still held on the bar. "My father's death is not something to make light of. Ensure Mr Lombard knows that. I don't know what research or information he digs up to make these events appear legitimate, but he's not to meddle in my personal affairs."

"My dear Miss Vale!" Nicholas caught hold of my hand and clasped it. "William is a legitimate paranormal investigator."

I yanked my hand away. "My father's ghost does not reside in this pub. And any spirits unearthed by your expert this evening won't be legitimate."

Nicholas tipped his head back and regarded me shrewdly. "A woman who speaks her mind. I like that."

"All women should be allowed to speak their mind."

His smile hardened. "Between you and me, I couldn't care less if the ghosts are real. As you can see, William has an obsessive fan base. My publishing house gets letters addressed to him every day. People beg him to visit their homes to communicate with the dead."

"What does he do to help such desperate types?"

"If the fee is substantial enough, he visits."

My top lip curled involuntarily. "Of course he does. And do you encourage such behaviour?"

"Any publicity William gets is wonderful for boosting book sales. And I always ensure the local press is around when he unearths a ghostly find." The amused glint in Nicholas's dark gaze revealed his lack of sincerity. "I believe you're here tonight in an official capacity, too. I trust you'll do the reading and investigation justice in the piece you write."

"The London Times publishes only the truth," I said.

"Yet I sense a bias from you. Even if a ghost sat beside you and told you all of your deepest, darkest secrets, you wouldn't believe such a thing was real."

"If a ghost floats over and shakes my hand as you have done, I'll be sure to print that. And get a photograph, too."

Nicholas's gaze tightened for a second, then he laughed. "After tonight, your opinion will change. William has met many cynics, and after they read his books and spend time with him, they become believers."

"I'm open-minded about most things. Ghosts aren't one of them. I want no trouble here." Perhaps it was because Nicholas had suggested my late father's spirit would be floating around the Craven Arms, but there was something about him that irked me. He was too smooth and confident.

Ever since he'd arrived at the pub, he'd marched around as if he owned the place. He even put Joe's back up by ordering him about, and Joe wasn't to be trifled with. As a former soldier, with battle scars to prove his bravery, he wasn't a man you wanted to get on the wrong side of. Even though he was almost forty-five, he had the energy and strength of a man half his age.

"If there's any trouble tonight, our noble vicar will banish it. I like to invite the local clergy to oversee things, just in case the spirits go from playful to vengeful." Nicholas gestured behind me.

I turned to discover Reverend Cecil Worthington had entered the pub. I was familiar with the vicar of All Hallows parish, but was surprised to see him at such an event. Close on his heels was a flustered Ruby Smythe. I'd expected my time tardy best friend to be her usual fifteen minutes late, but she'd added an extra half an hour for good measure, and left me waiting at the bar like a wallflower with only Benji for company. Although I didn't object, since he was such an excellent companion.

Her gaze darted around the crowd, and when she spotted me, she raised her hand, and I maneuvered over to her.

"Sorry! Sorry! Horse trouble. And Lady M trouble. When she heard I was attending a paranormal investigation, she gave me a list of dead relatives she expects me to speak to, and a bottle of holy water! I have no idea where she purchased that. It's most likely from the kitchen tap. What does she expect me to do with it? Drink it? Throw it over a ghost? Baptise the ghost hunter?"

"Lady M believes in ghosts?" I asked.

Ruby removed her hat and smoothed down her dark curls. "It would seem so. I can hardly take over the evening with her demands. But I'll need to, in order to get through this list. She knows so many dead people!"

"Lady M is well connected."

"And so dreadfully old."

"I'm glad you're here." Ruby always added fizz to the dullest situation.

"Who is your charming friend?"

I turned to discover Nicholas had followed me, and he was eyeing Ruby in an unpleasantly predatory manner. "Ruby Smythe, this is Nicholas Hawthorn. Mr Lombard's representative at the publishing house."

"Gosh. This is so exciting." Ruby shook his hand. "Do you get frightened, dealing with all these ghostly tales? Do any of the ghosts follow you home?"

Nicholas smiled indulgently, his gaze lingering on Ruby's fine figure, despite it being swathed in a long wool velour coat. "You get used to it. They're not scary. Some of the stories are even sad. The ghosts often have a message they'd like passed on and are unable to move on until they do."

Ruby blinked rapidly. "Goodness! Have you ever received a message?"

"I've not been blessed. William describes himself as the ghosts' conduit. He's a middleman between the living and the dead, but he can't always choose who talks to him."

"Has he ever been attacked by a ghost?" Ruby sounded a trifle breathless. "Do they touch him?"

"Please, tell me you're not serious," I muttered under my breath.

"William has had plenty of close encounters that would turn a lesser man's hair white," Nicholas said. "Stay for the whole evening, and you'll hear all about them. And perhaps we can speak privately later. I have wonderful stories to thrill you with. Do you like to be thrilled, my dear?"

Ruby blushed. "I—"

"We have plans. Thank you, Mr Hawthorn."

His gaze cut to me. "If you'll excuse me, I must see how our genius ghost hunter is doing. We can't keep his excited fans waiting for much longer." He bid us goodbye and headed around the back of the bar, where our esteemed author had taken a private room out of the way of the crowd to prepare himself.

We returned to the bar, and a patiently waiting Benji, who enthusiastically greeted Ruby.

"Is something wrong with your gin fizz?" Ruby asked after I'd taken a large sip.

"Joe makes a fine gin fizz," I said. "Why do you ask?"

Ruby gestured for Joe to come over. "Because of the sour look on your face."

I arched an eyebrow. "It's not the gin. It's the ghosts."

"Think of all the lovely money you'll donate to the dogs' home after this event is over."

"It's the only reason I'm doing it," I said.

Ruby's expression became shrewd. "There's more to it than that. What's got you rattled? You can't be unsettled about the possibility of ghosts. Most of the pubs your family owns are old and have fascinating histories. You must expect a few of the skeletons tucked away in the cupboards to rise and cause a ruckus."

"Skeletons don't rise. And, I'll have you know, all the closets, drawers, cupboards, and dressers in our pubs have been thoroughly cleaned." I sighed. "But you're right. There's something about this evening I don't like. It's unseemly to take money from people who want to communicate with a lost loved one. It's not possible. It feels wrong."

"The Spiritualist movement will tell you otherwise," Ruby said.

I looked around the crowded room again. Perhaps I was taking this too seriously. I should see the event as a fun evening of entertainment and nothing more. But it irritated me that Mr Lombard made his living this way.

"Sorry to keep you waiting." Joe finally arrived to serve Ruby. "The till hasn't stopped ringing since I opened the doors this evening. These ghost hunters love to drink."

Ruby ordered her usual martini and leaned in close. "Joe, have you ever seen a ghost in here?"

He tapped the side of his many times broken nose. "I believe in anything if it brings in a regular crowd like this, happy to spend their money."

"You will not take my family's name in vain!" The sharp, high-pitched tone of a young woman caught my attention, and I peered over people's heads to see what the kerfuffle was about.

Nicholas was speaking to a fierce-faced woman of no more than twenty. Her pale hair appeared damp, as if she'd just come in from outside. Her hands were in fists.

"What's that all about?" Ruby asked.

Before I could reply, the young woman shoved Nicholas, and he crashed to the floor.

Chapter 2

I grabbed Ruby's arm, and together, we shoved through the startled crowd, Benji beside me.

Nicholas was just getting to his feet and dusting down the back of his trousers, shooting an irritated look at the young woman. "There's no need for hysterics. I was simply explaining the situation. A situation you are well aware of."

"You're making a mockery of my great-grandmother. I won't have a dead relative exploited!" She took a step towards Nicholas, and he shuffled back.

Now I was closer to the woman, I saw fierce intelligence in her angry gaze as she stared down Nicholas.

"Nobody is being exploited, my dear." Nicholas straightened his jacket by tugging on the hem. "My client has many years of experience in the field of paranormal research. If your great-grandmother is here, you should stay. You may find the evening illuminating. She could have a message she wishes to pass on to you."

"I have a message to pass to your client," the woman spat back. "Leave the dead alone. They don't need to be disturbed. It's not welcome. My great-grandmother is gone, but she'd be rolling in her grave if she knew her memories were being exploited in such a distasteful manner."

"Paranormal research is never distasteful. It's a legitimate scientific exploration."

"Shame on you." The woman went to shove Nicholas again, but I stepped between them.

"Perhaps I may be of assistance," I said.

"Unless you can get this charlatan and his con artist author friend out of here, you're no good to me," the woman said.

"That is within my power," I said. "Veronica Vale. My family owns the Craven Arms. And you are?"

The young woman huffed out a breath, still glaring at Nicholas. "Millicent Baines. My great-grandmother was Jennifer Baines. And according to William Lombard, the biggest liar on this green earth, her ghost haunts your pub."

"Have you ever seen her?" Ruby asked, wide-eyed with interest.

"Of course not! Because she's dead. She has no reason to lurk around scaring people," Millicent said. "It's humiliating for my family to endure this spectacle."

"The crowd of curious onlookers thinks otherwise," Nicholas said. "They've paid to be here, so it would be unfair to deny them of a treat."

"You must! My great-grandmother's name will not be used as entertainment. She was a respectable lady. A pillion to the local Christian community. I will fight to ensure this event doesn't go ahead." Millicent raised a fist.

Benji trotted over and sniffed her other hand. She jerked back in surprise and then smiled.

"This is my companion, Benji," I said. "And I quite agree with you. We must never exploit the dead. They deserve every respect due to them."

Millicent stroked Benji, the tension leaching from her shoulders. "I have no issue with the book reading, although I can't believe anyone would entertain such nonsense. But when I heard there would also be a paranormal investigation to winkle out ghosts, I had to put a stop to things."

"I hadn't planned on permitting the event to take place." I glanced at Nicholas, a warning in my eyes to caution him to say nothing to inflame Millicent. "But the fee offered by the publishing house was so generous that I couldn't refuse."

Millicent's smile faded. "You're profiting from their lies?"

"If I were keeping the fee for myself, I'd agree it was wrong. But the money is for dogs like Benji," I said. "I volunteer at the dogs' home in Battersea. They do excellent work but are always short of money. The profits from this evening will go directly to charity."

Millicent's eyebrows rose. She looked down at Benji, who lifted a paw and cocked his head. "Oh! Well, I don't want to stop charity. My great-grandmother adored dogs, too. She had a Bichon Frise. Adorable little creature. Stocky and robust. She went everywhere with him. Even to France!"

"Your great-grandmother sounds like an adventurer," I said.

"She was. And a wonderful woman, but fiercely protective of the family's reputation. I'm most concerned her name will be called into question if this investigation takes place."

"She's not listed in this book." Ruby held up a copy of Mr Lombard's book. "The chapters are titled by pub name and the ghosts connected to them. The most prominent ghost discovered in the Craven Arms is the screaming nun."

"Great-grandmother wasn't a nun! Although she was a churchgoing woman," Millicent said.

"If you had allowed me to speak rather than pushing me over," Nicholas said, "I would have confirmed that although your relative gets a passing mention in the new publication, which has yet to be printed, William found little evidence to support her haunting the Craven Arms. He makes a brief comment about her colourful past, but that is all. Your concerns are for nothing."

There was something in his tone I didn't believe, but I wouldn't enrage Millicent again by pointing that out. "There you go. Your family's reputation won't be besmirched tonight."

"Of course, you never know who may come through," Nicholas said. "With so much excitable energy in one place, anything can happen and anyone can appear and reveal their secrets."

"How helpful. Weren't you going to see how Mr Lombard was doing? After all, you can't keep his fans waiting." I turned my back on Nicholas and his dreadfully ill-thought-out comment.

Nicholas harrumphed several times, then strode away.

"What an odious man," Millicent said.

"I quite agree." I kept my voice lowered even though the crowd stopped paying us attention. "And you'll be pleased to hear I charged him three times the usual rate to hire the pub. I had hoped such an extortionate fee would put him off, but he wouldn't be deterred."

"Good for you," Millicent said. "And with the money going to the dogs' home, my family can't disapprove too strongly. Although if great-grandmother is summoned, I'll haunt Mr Lombard myself when the time comes."

"You'd make a fearsome ghost."

She smiled. "I believe I would. I should go. I don't want to waste any more of my time."

"Why don't you stay for the evening?" I said. "Have a drink on me."

Millicent hesitated. "I should make sure Mr Lombard behaves. If his ghost hunting is as ludicrous as his book, he could end up claiming all sorts of nonsense."

"I'll also be on the lookout for any poorly worded claims. I need to ensure the Craven Arms's reputation doesn't take a beating." We headed back to the bar, and Millicent ordered a lemonade before slipping away into the crowd.

"Excuse me, I'd like to leave a gift for the author." A middle-aged woman in a sensible brown coat and flat shoes held out a bottle of wine to Joe.

Joe took the bottle. "I could give him a shout, and you could pass it to him. He's only out the back."

The woman's cheeks flushed, and she looked away. "No, thank you. I don't want to disturb him, and I need to get back to my seat." She scurried off.

Joe whistled as he inspected the bottle's label. "This is an expensive vintage. I need to change my career if you get gifts like this for summoning spirits."

"Goodness! That's quite a gift." It was a bottle of Château Lafite Rothschild.

Joe tucked the bottle underneath the bar. "Since this event is proving so popular, we could make it a regular thing. Have monthly ghost hunts."

"Let's draw a line under this one, I think," I said. "The Craven Arms performs well enough in terms of profits without turning it into a ghostly circus."

"You're the boss. What'll it be, vicar?" Joe asked.

Reverend Worthington had appeared by my side in his plain black cassock. "My usual sweet sherry, if you'd be so kind."

I nodded at him. "Good evening. I'm surprised to see you at such an event."

Reverend Worthington was a short man with a small pot belly. His thin, dark hair was accompanied by a weak chin and a warm smile. "I must remain stoical in matters such as these."

"Do you think you'll see a ghost tonight, Reverend?" Ruby asked.

"Belief is a powerful thing," he said. "And what a person believes can often come true."

"If that's the case, why am I not married to an obscenely wealthy man with a mansion in Mayfair?" Ruby asked. "I believe that to be true every day, yet here I am, slumming it in a tiny flat with dubious plumbing and sharing a bathroom with three other ladies."

Reverend Worthington chuckled politely as he accepted his sweet sherry from Joe and discreetly removed a peppermint from his mouth. "I find life is full of marvellous mysteries and miracles. And I'm always curious about how a person's beliefs and faith guide them through their life. God moves in mysterious ways."

Ruby frowned. "Do you have any tips for me to make my beliefs come true? At least get me my own bathroom. Could you put in a good word for me to the man upstairs?"

"Regular prayer and kind deeds are always welcomed by him. And he always listens."

Her cheeks coloured. "I have been a touch lapse on the prayer front of late. But I volunteer with Veronica when I can."

"Of course. At the dogs' home." Reverend Worthington bent to pat Benji. "That is kind of you. There are so many worthy causes that it can be hard to know which to focus upon. We have a regular soup kitchen at the church, but it always feels as if we need to do more."

"We all do what we can. It's good you're attending this event," I said. "There may be a few people who become unsettled by tonight's activities."

"That's true. And my door is always open to discuss matters of faith and the afterlife." Reverend Worthington picked up his sweet sherry. "We all need a guiding hand when dealing with death. If you'll excuse me." He ambled off into the crowd, pausing now and again to talk to people.

"Given tonight's book topic, he was remarkably calm," Ruby said.

"When you have a firm grip on your beliefs, there will be little to shake them."

She huffed out a breath. "Maybe the ghosts will reveal how I can snag myself a suitable man."

I softly laughed. "Providing they give you sensible advice, I have no issue with that."

We chatted and sipped our drinks, the minutes ticking by as Mr Lombard kept everybody waiting. Joe offered us a small glass of the wine he'd uncorked for our absent ghost expert. I declined, but Ruby had a few sips. She declared it most unpleasant.

Almost half an hour had passed, and I was considering marching off to haul Mr Lombard out of the back room to get on with the blasted book reading, when Nicholas appeared at the end of the bar and signalled to Joe.

They spoke for a few seconds, then Joe shrugged. He walked back to me. "Our esteemed author wants to make a grand entrance by having the lights turned off so he can sneak in. His publisher friend said it would be fun."

"Very dramatic," Ruby said. "Will he be wearing a billowing cape and top hat like a magician?"

"Having met the gentleman in question, nothing would surprise me," Joe said. "Is it a problem if I turn off the lights?"

"No, but make it quick," I said. "The sooner this debacle is over, the better."

Joe disappeared from behind the bar. A few seconds later, the lights blinked out.

There were several screams, a few gasps and mutters, and then an anticipatory silence spread throughout the bar.

Ruby fumbled for my hand. "I'm a little nervous."

"Boo," I whispered into her ear.

There was a rumble of something that sounded remarkably like thunder, followed by an eerie laugh that had several women shrieking.

"Good grief," I murmured. "Is this a stage performance?"

The lights sprang back on, blinding me, but after several blinks, I discovered William Lombard standing at the front of the crowd, looking immensely proud of himself and more than a touch smug.

Applause broke out, and people leapt to their feet, thrilled to find him there. He wore a luxurious black suit and crisp white shirt, his hair slicked back, and a smile on his face as he soaked up the welcome. Only after a good minute of applause did he make a gesture for quiet, and everyone settled into their seats, their rapt attention on Mr Lombard.

"Good evening, everybody. It's wonderful to see so many believers here." His voice was rich and warm. This man had made many public appearances and knew how to work a crowd. "Welcome to the Craven Arms. Let me take you on a haunting journey that'll make your spine shudder and your lips quiver."

I arched an eyebrow. "Is he reading from his new book or the latest Mills and Boon romance?"

Ruby stifled a laugh. "I know what I'd prefer. He does have a lovely voice, though."

Mr Lombard took in his expectant crowd, his gaze lingering on those in the front row. "Shall we begin by learning about the most haunted pub in London?"

Chapter 3

"The tragic woman's spectral cries are still heard when the moon is full and frost covers the grass outside the Craven Arms." Mr Lombard closed his notebook and peered expectantly at his enraptured audience. He'd been waxing lyrical about a lady murdered in cold blood by her jealous lover, and if his research was to be believed, she still haunted this place in search of revenge.

"What an intriguing tale," Ruby whispered in my ear.

"There's no grass outside the Craven Arms. The road has been a busy thoroughfare for almost a hundred years," I muttered in response.

"He makes it sound so real," Ruby said. "Are you sure you've never encountered this ghost?"

"I've got quite enough to deal with without searching for something that isn't real. The tale was too over the top to be true."

"It was dramatic, but enjoyable," Ruby said.

"The book is overwritten and factually incorrect. It sounds more like fiction than reality. And the evidence he's collected is his assumptions and imagination. Did

Mr Lombard take photographs? Did he interview any ghosts?"

"I don't think anyone has ever interviewed a ghost," Ruby said.

"My point exactly. You can't interview them or take their photograph because they don't exist."

Several women sitting near us tutted as they overheard our conversation.

"There are plenty more intriguing, haunting tales in my latest collection," Mr Lombard said. "And as an extra treat, I will be signing all books purchased during this evening's event. They'll be sure to keep you up at night."

Several of the ladies nervously tittered, most of them already clutching books ready to be signed.

Nicholas stood and joined Mr Lombard at the reading stand. "Thank you for a fascinating journey into the Craven Arm's ghostly past. We have time for questions if anybody would like to know more about the ghosts discussed this evening."

One of the few men in the audience stood from his seat. He was smartly dressed, middle-aged, with a neat black beard. "George Cloister. Local paranormal expert and fellow ghost hunter."

Mr Lombard's expression hardened for a second before his genial smile reappeared. "I thought you'd be too busy to attend tonight's hunt. I believe you're putting together your own collection of tales, aren't you?"

"As well you know, my second book is being considered for publication. And since I live within spitting distance of this pub, I consider this my patch." Mr Cloister's voice sounded weedy next to Mr Lombard's rich tones.

"I shall look forward to reading it. I enjoy your works of fiction."

"As do I yours. Although your fondness for wailing women suggests a disturbance in your psyche. Some trouble as a child, perhaps?"

The men dropped all attempts at civility and glowered at each other.

Nicholas cleared his throat. "Do you have a question you wish to ask?"

"I'm interested in your methods of recording." Mr Cloister adjusted his bowtie. "I use only the best during my studies. An Adams Reflex camera. It has a high degree of accuracy in capturing spectral essence for examination on film."

"That piece of equipment is overpriced and unreliable," Mr Lombard said.

"If you believe it to be so, what do you use, sir?"

"I find conversations with locals and spending several nights in a haunted location, detecting energy is more than adequate to gather quality data."

Mr Cloister tapped a finger against his chin. "The trouble with that method is we only have your word regarding your communications with the spirits."

"There's a man after my own heart," I murmured. "He's seen straight through this ruse."

"I use other tools to ensure accurate recording of all pertinent information pertaining to ghosts," Mr Lombard said. "The equipment is particular to my speciality. I designed it myself."

"How convenient," Mr Cloister said. "Has anyone tested the efficacy of such equipment?"

"This question time is to discuss ghosts, not equipment," Nicholas said. "Not all of us have a deep understanding of this technical methodology. Perhaps another member of the audience would like to learn more about the wailing woman? She captured my attention."

A lady stood, but Mr Cloister ignored her. "I visited another site where you claimed you'd seen a screaming nun. After putting money behind the bar, the landlord confirmed the nun didn't exist. He made up the story to boost trade and to play you for a fool. I'm afraid to say you've been made a laughingstock."

Mr Lombard looked around the crowd. "Yet I see no one laughing. Well, some of the ladies are laughing, but their titters are directed at you, old friend."

Mr Cloister's face flushed, and he glanced around before sinking into his seat.

"Who'd have thought there'd be rivalry in ghost hunting?" Ruby whispered. "It's such a particular activity."

"If there's money to be made in selling books and extracting funds from people who want to see a ghost, there'll be competition," I murmured.

"Have you ever met the ghost of a person you knew when they were alive?" a woman sitting in the front row asked Mr Lombard.

He switched on his charming façade as he turned his attention to her. "It's never happened, but I won't rule it out. I have a fascinating great uncle who was sent to Australia after some misdeeds. I've always wanted to talk to him about what trouble he got in and how he enjoyed life in Australia."

"Have you been scared by a ghost?" someone else asked.

"Ghosts are depicted as terrifying and creations to be frightened of, but that's because we don't understand them," Mr Lombard said. "They're something otherworldly, but that doesn't make them wrong or inappropriate. It means we need to get used to difference and become more accepting."

I grudgingly admitted he had a valid point. If people lived that way and treated others kindly, the world would be a far better place.

"Has a ghost ever chased you out of a building?" a woman asked.

"There have been times when my mettle was tested to the limits," Mr Lombard said. "But ghosts appreciate when a person is forthright. Whenever I enter a building to conduct an investigation, I clearly state why I'm there and encourage the ghost to communicate if they wish to do so. I also let them know they're under no pressure to speak to me."

Several ladies leaned forward in their seats, eager to hear more, and Mr Lombard's smile suggested he knew exactly what he was doing so he could captivate his audience.

"Sending messages and presenting themselves in visual form is taxing to a ghost's energy," he said. "Many ghosts aren't strong enough to be seen by us once they've passed."

The woman who'd handed the expensive bottle of wine to Joe raised a shaking hand.

Nicholas encouraged her to stand, but she remained seated. "If I wanted to talk to someone specific, do you have the power to do that?"

A flash of recognition lit Mr Lombard's eyes. "It's a question I'm often asked. People who have lost loved ones are desperate to say a few last words, especially if the passing was sudden and unexpected. Sadly, it's not always possible to communicate with all ghosts. Some pass straight over, while others linger. I've yet to discover the logic behind that. Why do some stay, and others go?"

"Unfinished business," Ruby whispered. "I have a few disrespectful former beaus I'd like to haunt and teach them a lesson."

I chuckled softly and settled into my seat as Mr Lombard continued answering questions. The woman who had raised her hand looked like she wanted to say more, but didn't have the courage to do so.

Ten minutes passed before Nicholas lifted his hand to quell the questions. "Thank you everyone. That's enough for this evening. We don't want to tire William before the main event. We'll have half an hour where you can buy your books and have them signed, and then our two-hour ghostly investigation begins."

"Can we buy a ticket for the investigation?" someone at the front of the audience asked.

"Sorry to disappoint, but this is an exclusive preview event. Only a select few were fortunate enough to receive an invitation to take part." Nicholas nodded at Mr Lombard. "Please show your appreciation for our spooky tale teller."

There was a burst of applause, and people formed an orderly queue as Mr Lombard settled behind a table, pen in hand, ready to sign his books.

"Do we have tickets to the exclusive investigation?" Ruby asked.

"I was given complimentary tickets," I said. "And I need to see this whole thing through so I can write a thorough article. While we wait, let's wander through the crowd and gather quotes. See what's got everyone so fascinated."

Ruby wrinkled her nose. "I need another drink. Meet you at the bar. Come on, Benji. Let's see if Joe has got pork scratchings for you."

Ruby went to fetch our drinks, while I spoke to several ladies, all enthusiastic about how wonderful William was and how excited they were to own copies of his books. None of them had a bad word to say about him, and several commented on how handsome he was. He wasn't unpleasant to look at, so I could see the appeal. But his chosen profession was morbid. Still, some people must say that about me. Writing about the dearly departed may seem morose, but I took comfort in crafting quality obituaries.

"Miss Vale." Nicholas gestured me over to the table where Mr Lombard was signing books. "You have three minutes with William."

"Three minutes to conduct an entire interview?" I asked.

"He's used to answering questions from journalists, so he won't waffle," Nicholas said. "And you were good enough to supply your questions in advance. Any that aren't tackled this evening will be returned to you by post. If you have any additional questions, now is your time to ask. The clock is ticking, and the ghosts wait for no man."

Mr Lombard glanced up as he returned a signed book to a happy ghost enthusiast. "I'm thrilled we were able to secure this location. I believe you own this establishment?"

I nodded. "My father bought a number of pubs around London and further afield."

"Do you have any more ghosts? I would be delighted to visit them."

I fixed Mr Lombard with a steely-eyed gaze. "As far as I'm aware, none of my pubs are haunted."

His smile was a touch smug. "That's the wonderful thing about ghosts. You don't know they're here unless they want you to know. Some call it sneaky, but I call it sensible. Why draw unwanted attention?"

I pulled out my notepad and flipped it open. "When did you first realise you had a talent for finding ghosts?"

"I've always been what my mother called 'sensitive.' Even when I was a child, she'd catch me talking to thin air. But I've always been able to see things no one else can."

"Remarkable. Have you considered having your eyes examined? They can do wonderful things with glasses, these days."

Mr Lombard held up a hand as Nicholas protested. "Miss Vale is allowed to be sceptical. Most people are when it comes to the supernatural. A mind that doesn't question is a dull instrument. And I see nothing dull about Miss Vale."

I nodded at the compliment.

He signed another book. "I've spent my life either being ridiculed or adored. Ghosts bring out extreme reactions."

"You have an adoring audience tonight," I said. "Apart from Mr Cloister. He appears to be a rival."

Mr Lombard paused before signing another book and murmuring a thank you. "There will always be up-and-comers who claim to be the next expert. George has learned a lot from me. I met him on a ghost hunt a few years ago. It was his first. The unfortunate fellow was so terrified he only stayed half an hour before fleeing into the dark."

"Why does he remain interested in ghosts if they're so terrifying?" I asked.

"Ghosts are a source of fascination, not fear." Mr Lombard shooed Benji away when he ambled over to sniff his knee. "I have allergies."

I called Benji to my side. "What's the most important skill needed to be a successful ghost hunter? A healthy imagination?"

"Patience. And learning to embrace the boredom. I once spent two weeks in an abandoned abbey in darkest Wales in search of the white woman. A ghostly creature shaped of shadowy mist. She only appears to people she trusts. She'd been treated terribly when alive, so I understood her hesitancy."

"Did the ghost deem you trustworthy enough to show herself?" Even though I was entirely sceptical, I was a little bound up in the extreme tale.

"On the final night, just after the stroke of midnight, when I'd admitted defeat and was packing my things because snow was forecast, she appeared. She stared at me for ten seconds without blinking before vanishing. I didn't breathe the whole time. It was remarkable."

"Remarkable, indeed! Did you take a photograph? Is she in your new book?"

"The account of the sighting has its own entry." Mr Lombard signed another book and handed it over. "Sadly, ghosts rarely appear in photographs."

"How convenient," I murmured.

"Not for those who desire to document them. Even if I could capture a ghost in a photograph, there would still be those who refused to acknowledge the truth." Mr Lombard lifted an eyebrow and gave me a searching look.

"Photographs can be manipulated. We get sent incredible things at the newspaper. Many of them have been falsified in the hopes of receiving payment."

"How disappointing. Will you be joining us for the rest of the evening?" Mr Lombard asked. "Perhaps your mind will be opened by the truth."

"I wouldn't miss it," I said. "My article won't be complete if I don't experience everything."

His eyes narrowed a fraction. "I shall look forward to reading it."

I found Ruby waiting at the bar with our drinks, and we settled in, while Mr Lombard finished the book signing and then addressed more of his adoring female fans.

"Who's joining us on the ghost hunt?" Ruby asked.

"Not me," Joe said from behind the bar as he collected empty glasses. "I'll be around, but I'll stay here to keep an eye on things. We don't want troublemakers coming in and disturbing the fun, do we?"

"I have a ticket for the investigation." The nervy woman who'd gifted the wine stood behind Ruby. "I go to as many of William's investigations as I can afford to."

I introduced myself and Ruby.

She responded with a nervous smile. "I'm Grace Vilein."

"Do you believe in ghosts?" I asked.

"I believe there's more to this life than we can understand," Grace said earnestly. "Just because we can't see something doesn't mean it's not there."

"I'm all for having an open mind," Ruby said. "And ignore Veronica's sceptical air. I'm rather excited about this evening."

Grace smiled, but had trouble maintaining eye contact. She quickly excused herself and sat in the corner, nursing a small glass of bitter lemon.

We waited by the bar until most of the people from the book reading had left, until the only ones remaining were Mr Lombard, Joe, Grace, Mr Cloister, Reverend Worthington, me, Ruby, and Benji.

"I'll lock the main door, shall I?" Joe asked Nicholas.

Before he had a chance to slide the bolt into place, Millicent barged in. "I'm not too late, am I?"

"Do you have a ticket for tonight's investigation?" Nicholas asked.

"No, but I'll pay for it now." She fumbled in her pocket. "I was told I could stay. Miss Vale said I could."

"I'm sorry, my dear, but tickets must be bought in advance. And we can only have a select few for a preview investigation. If the number is too large, the ghosts become agitated and refuse to appear. This is a scientific investigation. We can afford no mistakes. I must ask you to leave." Nicholas was taking great delight in refusing Millicent.

Millicent scowled and looked at me.

"Surely we can allow one more person," I said.

"Absolutely not," Nicholas said. "And given the fee you've received for tonight's event, you'd be wise not to interfere."

Ruby squeezed my arm, and I held my tongue. Benji growled softly.

Millicent let out an exasperated sigh, then stomped out of the pub.

"Why would she want to be here?" Ruby whispered to me.

"To ensure Mr Lombard doesn't fake her great-grandmother's ghost."

Once the doors were locked, we gathered in a small circle in front of Mr Lombard, Nicholas, standing beside him. Even though there was no such thing as ghosts, I felt a tickle of nervous excitement. What delights and frights were in store for us?

Mr Lombard smiled warmly and rubbed his hands together. "Is anyone here of a nervous disposition or has a heart condition?"

I glanced at Grace, but she remained silent.

"Excellent. To maximise the likelihood of a visitation, this investigation must be conducted in the dark. Is everybody ready to welcome in the Craven Arm spirits?"

Chapter 4

"I thought this would be more entertaining?" Ruby muttered in my ear, her hand on my elbow, so she knew where I was.

"I never said tonight would be entertaining," I replied.

"I expected some fun. It's freezing! And I can't feel my toes."

"Are the ghosts numbing your extremities?"

"It's got nothing to do with the pub's ghosts! It's these heels. I should have kept my riding boots on. They're insulated and flat-heeled."

"Listen carefully, everybody." Mr Lombard's tone was hushed. He'd been leading us around in the gloom for an hour. "I heard ghostly laughter ahead of us. Everybody be deathly quiet."

"Nobody is laughing," Ruby whispered. "Ghost hunting is dull."

Someone shushed Ruby, but in the darkness, I couldn't see who it was.

"The only thing that's keeping me going is knowing there's a bottle of brandy behind the bar," Ruby muttered. "That will warm me up."

We waited in silence. No laughter, ghostly or otherwise, could be heard.

Benji whimpered as we continued along the dark upstairs passageway in the Craven Arms.

"Your dog senses something," Mr Cloister said, his voice so close to my ear it made me jump.

I leaned away from him. "Benji is unsettled because it's dark."

"He's been whimpering at regular intervals. To an expert such as myself, that means something."

"It means he's in need of supper and his bed," I said. "As am I."

"William will report his behaviour as evidence," Mr Cloister murmured. "Animals are sensitive to spirits."

"He can leave Benji's name out of his scribblings," I said. "My dog isn't a ghost sensitive. He's far too sensible."

Although the lights were out in the entire building, I could make out the dark shapes of the other ghost hunters. Mr Lombard led the way as our resident expert. Grace and Reverend Worthington were in front of me and Ruby, while Mr Cloister was at the back of the group with Nicholas.

So far, other than Mr Lombard pretending to hear strange noises and laughter, we'd happened across nothing suspicious. Certainly nothing that couldn't be explained as entirely normal.

"We could sneak to the bar and ask Joe to open the brandy early," Ruby whispered. "Get a jump on everyone else."

"He's most likely got his feet up in the back, having a nap," I said. "Best we don't disturb him."

"I'll use my ghost detection camera," Mr Lombard announced. "I'm hopeful of an apparition at any moment. Listen for strange sounds, so I know which direction to take the photographs."

Someone's stomach gurgled, and several people laughed.

Three sharp taps sounded behind us, and I jumped and turned around. Of course, I could see nothing.

"That's a sign!" Grace whispered. "Ghosts tap to communicate. I read about it in William's book."

"What do the tappings mean?" Ruby asked.

The noise continued. A soft tap-tap-tap.

"This is excellent," Mr Lombard said. "First contact. Nobody make any sudden moves. The ghost must learn to trust us, so it knows we're no threat."

"Can you see it?" Grace asked.

"Not yet. This spirit may not have the energy to materialise. We should be content with it tapping its requests." Mr Lombard brushed past me, holding something out in front of him.

"It's Nicholas tapping his request that the evening comes to an end," I whispered to Ruby. "He's as bored as you are."

"I heard that, my dear," Nicholas said.

I was glad it was dark because my cheeks flushed at being caught being snippy. I'd been certain he'd snuck off to rap on a piece of wood to scare us.

"Spirit, we mean you no harm," Mr Lombard said. "We're believers, and we'd like to help you. Do you have a message for us?"

There was no reply.

"Spirit, I ask you again. We come as friends of the other side. What would you like to tell us?"

"The ghost is probably tired and telling us to leave it alone," Ruby said. "It has made its home here, and it doesn't want strangers nosing about and asking ridiculous questions."

"I thought you were excited by the prospect of meeting a ghost?" I asked.

"It's less glamourous than I thought it would be. And I'm so cold."

"Let's keep moving. Give the spirit our energy." Mr Lombard encouraged us along as he took photographs in the dark, a regular click the only indication he was hard at work.

We traipsed along the upstairs corridor for twenty minutes, peeking into various rooms as Mr Lombard called to the ghost, and the ghost refused to answer. He strode around, holding his ghost capturing camera. I was uncertain how it worked, since he wasn't using a flash.

There was another thump, this time below us.

"This way! Follow me." Mr Lombard bumped into me as he chased the ghost. "Our spirit friend is on the move. She must want to show us something."

"Now it's a she?" Ruby asked. "Did I miss something?"

We dashed after Mr Lombard and down the rickety wooden staircase into the main bar. He lit a candle and held it high, casting long shadows around the room as the flame flickered. A small pile of books leftover from the signing had been knocked over and were strewn across the floor.

"Incredible! This is a clear sign of ghostly activity." Mr Lombard passed the candle to Nicholas, then held his camera over the books and took several photographs. He winced, set down the camera, and flexed his fingers before shaking them out. "Everybody gather around and search for cold spots. That's a sign a ghost is near."

We stood around the books, and I felt vaguely ridiculous as I held my hands out.

"Every spot is cold," Ruby whispered. "How do we find the ghostly cold? Does it feel different to regular cold?"

"It feels icy here." Mr Cloister was crouched over the books, peering intently at the floor.

"That would be due to the gaps in the wooden floorboards," I said. "There's a cellar beneath us where Joe stores the barrels and bottles. When you're not standing on a rug, you feel the chill."

Mr Cloister and Mr Lombard ignored me and spent several minutes inspecting a spot on the floor and taking photographs, their previous animosity gone as they shared their interest.

"We must access the cellar. There could be a body buried down there," Mr Lombard said.

"I assure you, none of my cellars have bodies buried in them," I said. "And it's not safe to wander down there in the dark. You could damage my stock."

Mr Lombard finally looked up at me. "It's no matter. I've arranged a lone vigil in there shortly."

My eyebrows lifted. He hadn't arranged it with me.

After several more minutes of hunting for cold spots, the group slowly lost interest.

Mr Lombard must have sensed he was losing his crowd, because he rapped his knuckles on the bar to get our attention. "That's enough excitement. It's time for some refreshments. Somebody, turn on the lights."

Since I knew the pub layout better than everyone else, I used the bar to feel my way along to the wall and switched on the main lights. Everyone blinked like startled kittens as our eyes adjusted. The pub looked the same as always. If a ghost had been here, other than knocking over some books, it had left no mark. I was hoping for at least a splash of ectoplasm.

I strode over to Mr Lombard. "What's this about a lone vigil in my cellar?"

He inspected his camera. "I arranged it with your landlord. He said, providing I was careful I could go down there on my own. It's important to have focus when summoning spirits."

"What will you be doing to summon the spirits?"

"I'll sit in a meditative state and open myself to them. It takes intense concentration, so it's best done alone. Once I've brought forth enough energy, a ghost could manifest for everybody to see."

I was unhappy about this arrangement. "You should have someone with you. The cellar steps are old, and there are low ceilings down there, so it's easy to bump your head."

"I'll be fine. Nicholas inspected the space and considered it suitable. And your landlord showed me around when I arrived. I'll be careful. I do know what I'm doing." His smile was a touch condescending. "And I only need half an hour. While I'm down there, everyone can relax and have some light refreshments. It's included in the ticket price."

"I'm all for refreshments." Ruby joined us. "I need a hot toddy after all that running about looking for ghosts. Do you think you've captured anything on your camera?"

"I'll need to develop the film. It's infrared, so it only captures ghost energy."

How hard I fought not to roll my eyes.

Joe ambled out of the back room and greeted us. "Drinks all round? And the food is over on that table, if you'd like to help yourselves."

Ruby dashed over, and I heard her cajoling him into making her a special hot toddy alongside a small glass of brandy.

"If I may have your attention for a moment," Mr Lombard called out. "I'll be in the cellar for approximately half an hour, communing with the dead. While you wait, please browse the remaining books on display. And remember, I'm happy to sign any copies purchased this evening."

"May we come down with you?" Grace had her hands clasped together.

"This part of the investigation is only suitable for professionals. I assure you, I'll reveal my findings as soon as possible."

"Sit with me and enjoy a sandwich," Reverend Worthington said to Grace. "I've had quite enough excitement for one evening, so I'm sure you have, too."

Grace looked disappointed, but didn't object to the reverend's kind offer.

"Don't worry if you hear strange sounds coming from the cellar." Mr Lombard pulled a handkerchief from his pocket and dabbed his forehead. "The ghosts make odd noises, so moans and groans are to be expected. I'll be perfectly safe. And as soon as I have something of interest, I'll request the door is unlocked, and you can all look."

Joe walked over and handed me a hot toddy, his face creased with concern. "Ruby said you're angry about that fellow. I told Mr Lombard he needed to check with you about using the cellar for his ghostly business, but he said he had."

"Then he's not been truthful with either of us." I inhaled the heady, spicy scent of the toddy. "But I see no harm in it. Mr Lombard said he'd examined the cellar to ensure it was safe to conduct his investigation."

"He only glanced down the steps. The other chap, Nicholas, he came down with me and looked around. Spent ages poking about. I thought he was up to something."

"Most likely, planting ghostly clues in an attempt to fool us," I said.

"I'll unlock the cellar," Joe said. "And make sure there's nothing down there he'll trip over."

Everyone settled at tables, and I was sipping my toddy, grateful for its warmth, when Benji's ears pricked and he darted away. Never one to ignore my dog, I followed him. Benji led me along the corridor that ran parallel to the bar, and he stopped in front of Millicent, who was hiding behind a pile of wooden crates.

"What are you doing back here?" I asked.

She stepped out, frowning. "Did you see her?"

"You're asking about your ghostly great-grandmother?"

Millicent nodded. "I couldn't bear the thought of her name being misused for this charade. Did they do something? Make a fake ghost to mock her? I hope it wasn't convincing."

Ruby's heels tapped behind me as she joined us. "What's this?"

"We have an extra guest," I said to Ruby. "All we heard were a few taps and books got knocked over. It was nothing remarkable. Certainly nothing I would put down to a ghost being present."

"We wandered about in the dark for ages, getting cold and thirsty," Ruby said. "This will be my first and last ghost investigation."

"Nicholas won't be happy you snuck back in," I said to Millicent. "Not after you treated him so roughly."

"That's why I'm hiding! Mr Hawthorn is a jumped-up little man, who only cares about how fat his wallet is. It's my family they're exploiting, so I have every right to be here."

I couldn't be cross with Millicent for wanting to know what these charlatans were doing. I'd be the same if a member of my family was having their ghost dragged through the spectral mud.

"Mr Lombard is about to venture into the cellar," I said. "Why don't you sneak off before anyone else discovers you?"

"What's he doing down there? He'd better not be bothering my great-grandmother."

"He's attempting a ghost summoning, so he'll return empty-handed," I said.

Millicent scowled, then sighed. "You're right. I should leave. Mr Hawthorn will only scold me if he sees me. You won't say I was hiding back here, will you?"

"It's as if you're a ghost. Invisible to the human eye. I assume you came through the back entrance?" I asked.

Millicent nodded. "Thank you. No need to show me out. I know the way."

I returned to the main bar with Ruby and Benji and called Joe over. "I'd like a word with you."

"In need of another hot toddy?"

"Not yet. Two things. Did Nicholas pay you to knock over those books and tap on wood to frighten us while we were creeping about in the dark?"

Joe rubbed the back of his neck and wouldn't meet my gaze. "He said it would be fun and make the night more entertaining. I meant no harm by it."

"Joe! How could you?" Ruby exclaimed. "There I was, thinking we had a ghostly friend, and it was you all along."

"You thought no such thing," I said.

Ruby laughed. "At least let me pretend. Joe, you're a stinker."

"I'm sorry. I didn't think anyone would take this evening seriously." Joe glanced at Grace and the vicar. "No one really believes in ghosts, do they?"

"Some of us make an excellent living from those beliefs." Mr Lombard walked over with an almost empty glass of red wine in one hand. "Perhaps you'd like to purchase a copy of my book? It's full of factual information and scientific proof about ghosts."

Joe shook his head. "I'm not much of a reader."

Mr Lombard held out his glass for a refill, then ambled off towards the cellar entrance. "Everyone, your attention, please. I'm entering the cellar. I shall soon return with news. Lock me in, will you?" He drained his glass and turned to Joe.

Joe hurried over with a key in hand, and let Mr Lombard into the cellar before returning to the bar and placing the key on a shelf. "What was the other thing, Veronica?"

"Did you let Millicent back into the pub during the ghost hunt?"

"I hope she's not here." Nicholas marched over. "She's been an absolute thorn in my side ever since I arranged this investigation."

Joe shrugged. "I felt sorry for her. She's only young, and she got upset when I said she couldn't come in. I let her in through the back door and told her to be quick. Millicent only wanted to see what was going on, and she promised she wouldn't cause trouble."

"It's agitators like Millicent who give ghost investigations a bad name." Mr Cloister joined in the conversation. "They stir trouble. If they took the time to understand what was going on, they would become believers, too. I explain it all in my own book. Let me get you a copy. I always carry several with me." He hurried away.

Joe grimaced. "He's not going to make me read from it, is he?"

"You should. It can be your punishment for pretending to be a ghost," I said.

Joe gulped. "I'm not in trouble, am I? I thought nothing would come of it."

I patted his arm. "Nothing has come of it. But don't let Nicholas or Mr Lombard fool you again. And don't always believe a young lady when she blinks up at you with tears in her lashes."

Ruby nodded sagely. "We're very good at knowing how to twist men around our little fingers."

"Sorry, Veronica. It won't happen again."

I settled into a seat with Ruby opposite me and Benji by my side, making a few notes for my article. We'd just finished our hot toddies when the lights blinked out again.

Ruby squeaked. "Was that the ghost, or is Joe still teasing us?"

"I'm plumping for Joe." I set down my pencil and waited for the lights to come back on.

"Don't worry, everyone," Joe called out. "This is an old building, and the electrics can be peculiar."

"Because of the ghosts," Grace said in the dark.

"I've got candles out the back. I won't be a minute." Joe's footsteps thumped away.

Benji rested his head on my knee, and I gave him a reassuring pat. Not that he needed it. He was always calm in moments of crisis.

There was a soft creak, a gasp, and then a wheeze.

"Is that a ghost or someone struggling for air?" Ruby whispered.

I strained to listen to the odd wheezing sound, but in the dark, I couldn't pinpoint its location.

"Help! Will somebody help me?"

"That sounded like Mr Lombard," Ruby said.

There was another wheeze, then a loud thump.

I stood and felt my way to the cellar door. I tried to open it, but it was locked. I struck it with my hand. "Mr Lombard, are you all right in there?"

There was silence.

"More ghostly business?" Ruby's voice in my ear made me jump.

"Joe, where are those candles?" I asked.

"Right here! Give me a second to light one."

"I need the cellar door unlocked," I said. "Something's happened to Mr Lombard."

A match was struck, and several candles lit. Joe swiftly handed them around before unlocking the cellar door.

As we peered into the gloom, long shadows stretching before us, we discovered Mr Lombard lying at the bottom of the stone steps.

Chapter 5

After the initial shock of seeing Mr Lombard sprawled on his back, I was the first to spring into action. I hurried down the stone steps, closely followed by Benji and Ruby.

I crouched beside Mr Lombard, but his unblinking eyes told me the unfortunate truth as I checked his pulse. There were no signs of life.

There was a faint whiff of something in the air I couldn't place. I leaned over the body and sniffed close to his mouth. All I detected was the faint aroma of alcohol.

"How's he doing?" Joe called from the top of the stairs.

"Mr Lombard is dead." I held the candle high and peered around the cellar, but we were alone.

Reverend Worthington crept down the stairs, his expression solemn. "Was he of a particular faith?"

I looked up the stone stairs. "I didn't know the man. Where's Nicholas?"

"He wanted some air and a smoke, so I sent him outside." Joe followed behind Reverend Worthington. "Cor blimey! Mr Lombard is really dead?"

I nodded. "I'm no expert, but it's possible he broke his neck when he took a tumble."

"These stairs are uneven," Reverend Worthington said. "He could have stumbled down them."

"There's nothing wrong with my stairs, provided you're careful," Joe said gruffly.

"I'll say a prayer over him." Reverend Worthington bowed his head and murmured quietly.

"Mr Lombard must have gotten disorientated in the dark." Ruby's tone was hushed. "That kept happening to me when we were upstairs. I thought I was heading in one direction and then hit a wall. I bruised my knees."

"Why did he call out for help?" I asked.

"Perhaps he felt unwell?" Ruby suggested. "Or something scared him, and he panicked. He fled up the steps but then realised the door was locked. He cried out because he wanted to escape, but he was caught."

"Caught by what?"

Ruby looked around with wide eyes. "Well, he's a ghost hunter. Maybe the ghosts didn't like him poking around the Craven Arms. They taught him a lesson."

"Nonsense. But whatever happened, we need the police here." I stood from my crouched position, took one more look around the cellar, and then headed back up the steps with everybody else. "Joe, keep the door shut and make sure nobody comes down here."

He nodded and shooed everyone out of the way before locking the door. What was left of the party huddled together, not seeming to know what to do.

"And would you call the police, please?" I asked him.

His expression soured. "If I must. This was Mr Lombard's fault, though. He was alone down there."

"They will still need to know what happened."

Joe grumbled a few words under his breath, then hurried out to the back corridor, where the pub's only telephone was located.

Someone stumbled and there was a thud, followed by a curse. Nicholas loomed into view, rubbing his shin.

"There's been an incident." I caught hold of his arm to ensure I had his full attention. "Mr Lombard has had a fall."

"Decided to take a nip of brandy from your stores, I suppose." Nicholas's chuckle died when I didn't join in. "Whatever's the matter?"

"He fell down the stone steps. I'm sorry, he's dead."

Nicholas jerked away from me. He paced beside the bar, not looking happy.

"I'm sorry for your loss," Ruby held her candle up high.

He looked up at her. "It's not that."

Ruby glanced at me, eyebrows lifted. "You weren't close? I assumed you had a professional relationship."

"William said this investigation was what he needed to get his latest book finished. Damn and blast it!" Nicholas scowled at a pile of hardback books. "The last thing I need is a dead author and an unfinished book on my hands. Although ... if we put a spin on it and say a ghost shoved him down the stairs, it would boost sales."

"I'm glad you can see the positive in such a tragic situation," I said.

Nicholas was unperturbed by my sharpness. "We all have to make our living. William would want his final book published, and his fans will be eager to get their hands on it, especially when they discover a ghost killed him."

Grace staggered into me and would have hit the floor if I hadn't caught her. She lay in my arms in a dead faint.

"Poor old thing." Ruby fanned Grace's pale face as she peered at her in the candlelight. "She clearly admired Mr Lombard. She must be in shock."

"Help me with her." I passed my candle to Reverend Worthington and adjusted my grip on Grace.

Ruby and I carried Grace to a chair and propped her up. I leaned over her and lightly tapped her cheek. It took several firm taps before she roused.

"You're quite safe. You fainted. How do you feel?" I asked.

Grace looked around the pub, her eyes bleary. "Do you see him?"

"To whom are you referring?"

"William! If he were able to, he'd return as a ghost. He'd want everybody to know the truth about the afterlife." Her gaze darted as she searched for Mr Lombard's elusive ghostly form.

Ruby's mouth hung slightly open as she also looked around. "I hadn't thought about that, but it makes sense. He wouldn't want to hide such important information from people. After all, this was his life's work."

"That's untrue." Mr Cloister lingered close by. "William worked in sales. He sold Bibles to people on their doorsteps."

Grace appeared confused. "I... I don't understand. In his first book, he wrote that he dedicated his life to the supernatural. Ever since he was a child, he had a special ability to see things others couldn't. He wouldn't waste that on selling Bibles."

"Spreading the word of our Lord is never a waste of time," Reverend Worthington said soothingly.

Grace's hand fluttered against her chest as her eyes filled with tears. "Sorry! No, of course not. Forgive me, Reverend. I didn't mean to sound disrespectful. I'm so surprised by what's happened."

"You shouldn't believe everything you read," Mr Cloister said. "Certainly not when those words were written by a charlatan. May Willian rest in peace."

Nicholas shrugged. "We spun his words and experiences to ensure people bought the books."

"You had your doubts about his work?" I stood after a final check on Grace.

Nicholas pulled out a packet of cigarettes. "After all these years, William has never given me a pinch of proof that ghosts are real."

"Why publish work if you know it to be false?" I asked.

"I deal in fiction and nonfiction. It makes no difference to me if what's on the page is real or not, providing it sells plenty of copies." Nicholas returned to his pacing. "What a mess he's left me. I'll have to get a ghostwriter to finish the book. How's that for irony?"

"If you're looking for a capable chap, I'm your man." Mr Cloister followed Nicholas like an eager puppy, looking for a treat.

He regarded him shrewdly. "We can talk about it another time."

"At a more appropriate time," I added.

Joe returned from making his telephone call. "The police are on their way. They put me through to an Inspector Jacob Templeton. He said they won't be long."

"Good. I'm glad your inspector is involved," Ruby said. "It makes life easier when we don't have to introduce ourselves to a new detective and explain how useful we are."

"Inspector Templeton rarely considers either of us useful." My ongoing fractious relationship with Inspector Jacob Templeton came in peaks and troughs. One day, we'd rub along quite nicely, and the next, we'd bicker like an old married couple who never liked each other in the first place. It was a vexing relationship to find oneself in. I wished the man would see sense and realise what an asset I was to his work. Add in the excellent abilities of my wonderful dog, and the charm and determination of my best friend, and Inspector Templeton had serious talent on his side.

"Joe, could you see about the lights?" Ruby asked. "We don't want any more ghosts to get us."

"I'll get right on it." He stomped off, and a moment later, the lights came back on, causing several gasps and relieved sighs. Joe returned. "They'd been turned off!"

"By a ghost or a human hand?" I murmured to Ruby.

She nudged me with an elbow. "Let's see what the police have to say about the matter."

While we waited for them to arrive, I sat with Ruby, Benji, Reverend Worthington, and Grace, and observed everybody.

Grace appeared genuinely shaken, her body trembling. Joe appeared mildly confused as he tidied the bar and topped up people's drinks. Mr Cloister looked excited, most likely because he had the prospect of adding his mark to Mr Lombard's final book. Reverend

Worthington was in a world of his own as he sucked on a peppermint and took tiny sips from his sweet sherry.

"Nicholas has slunk off again," I said to Ruby.

"The last time I noticed him, he was talking to Mr Cloister. Do you think he's fled the scene of the crime? You are thinking a crime has been committed?"

"We need to consider all options, and we need to watch Nicholas. His only interest is how much money he can make. And he said himself, Mr Lombard's death, when cast in a particularly crass light, ensures the new book will sell like fresh loaves out of the bakery on Old Church Street."

"He'd have to be cold-hearted to think he can get away with this," Ruby said.

"Perhaps he is. We need to find out. I'll be back in a moment." I joined Joe at the bar. "Is Millicent still here?"

"As far as I know, she left the same way I snuck her in," Joe said. "Through the tradesman's entrance."

"Did you see her leave?" I asked. "She said she would, but I was otherwise occupied, so I didn't see her go."

Joe shook his head. "I was busy with the drinks. She could still be here. Do you want me to check out the back?"

"In a moment. Where do you normally keep the key to the cellar?"

"Behind the bar. On the shelf over here. I always put it in the same place because I lose it otherwise, and then get moaned at when I can't get in the cellar to change the empty barrels."

"And you definitely locked Mr Lombard in the cellar?"

"That's right. He told me to. I checked the door. It was sealed shut."

"And then you put the key back in its usual place." It wasn't a question. I'd seen him do it.

Joe nodded. "Why do you ask?"

"Putting the pieces into place," I murmured.

A knock on the front door drew our attention, and Joe hurried over to unlock it. Inspector Jacob Templeton stepped inside. He was accompanied by two uniformed policemen. His gaze went around the room, and he took everyone in.

He stopped at me and sighed as he walked over. "What a surprise. There's been a murder in one of your pubs, and you're already here. Are you psychic?"

I smiled. "I assure you, I'm not. However, inspector, do you believe in ghosts?"

Chapter 6

I fixed Inspector Templeton with a stern look when he didn't answer my question.

"You aren't joking?" he finally said.

"Death is never something to make a joke of. However, in this case, you'll have to wade through some ghostly theories to retrieve the truth."

Inspector Templeton's eyes narrowed. "Where is the body?"

"Still in the cellar. We haven't touched Mr Lombard. Well, I checked his pulse to determine if he was alive. The entrance is over there." I pointed to the doorway, and Joe took them to the door and unlocked it for them.

We waited while they went down, only the occasional scuff of a boot signaling anyone was moving beneath our feet.

The lights flickered overhead.

"Ghosts often interfere with electrical items." Mr Cloister stood watching the entrance to the cellar.

"I prefer to think it's the mice chewing on the wires," Joe murmured.

A moment more of waiting, and Inspector Templeton re-emerged from the cellar with the two policemen. He introduced himself to the assembled group. "We'll need to take statements from all of you."

"We won't be of any use," Mr Cloister said. "William was in the cellar on his own. He insisted on being alone to commune with the ghosts."

Inspector Templeton drew in a breath, and his gaze flicked to me. "Even so, one of you may have seen or heard something useful. A clue to help us figure out what happened. We won't hold you any longer than necessary. We'll start by taking names and addresses."

While everyone took a seat and waited their turn to be interviewed, Inspector Templeton walked over to me and Ruby. "Talk me through this evening's events."

"It's very much as Mr Cloister said," I replied.

"When I spoke to your landlord on the telephone, he informed me there was a ghost hunt going on?"

"William Lombard was an expert in the paranormal," I said. "He hired the Craven Arms to do a reading and then sign some books. He then held an exclusive preview event for a few of us to conduct an actual ghost hunt."

Inspector Templeton paused in his note-taking. "And did you see any ghosts?"

"Inspector, you know there's no such thing. We walked around in the dark, then came to the bar for refreshments. Mr Lombard announced he would go into the cellar on his own and call forth the spirits."

"By that time, the only spirit I was interested in was Joe's excellent brandy," Ruby said. "We were waiting here when the lights went out."

"My apologies for listening in." Mr Cloister crept over. "As I keep saying to everybody, ghosts affect electrical items. William was interfering with matters he didn't understand. He angered a ghost, and it tripped the electrical fuses and attacked him in the dark."

"If you could find me this ghost, I'd be pleased to interview it," Inspector Templeton said without a trace of irony in his voice.

Mr Cloister's eyebrows flashed up. "Records show ghosts can be violent. Poltergeists, in particular, are impossible to control."

"I'm focused on the living witnesses for now," Inspector Templeton said. "Did Mr Lombard arrange this evening?"

"His publisher, Nicholas Hawthorn, was in charge of the particulars," I said.

"He slipped out the back to have a cigarette," Mr Cloister said.

"No one is allowed to leave." Inspector Templeton instructed an officer to collect Nicholas, then he led me a short way from the main group, his hand firm on my elbow. "What do you think happened? Was it an accident, death by human hand, or a malevolent ghost?"

"Inspector Templeton can't seriously be considering the option that a ghost killed that fellow." My younger brother, Matthew, sat on the end of my mother's bed the next morning. In one hand, he held half a piece of buttered toast, and in the other, he cradled a long-limbed puppy that was half-asleep.

"He doesn't. He was teasing me." I sat on the other side of the bed, an empty bowl of porridge beside me. I'd spent the last half an hour eating with my family, reflecting on last night's alarming events and who could be involved.

"You must read this and then pass it to Inspector Templeton." My mother had a copy of one of Mr Lombard's books open on the bedsheets. "It says here spirits are vengeful. Those who leave this earthly plane with unfinished business hold grudges, so it's impossible for them to pass. They linger like unhappy shadows, gathering energy until they're strong enough to strike."

"A vengeful spirit struck no one," I said. "The death was most likely due to a fall."

"I know that look." Matthew leaned over and dropped his toast crust into my bowl. "You think there's more to the story than that?"

I lifted one shoulder. "Maybe a vengeful person was involved, but not a ghost. Mr Lombard has been pretending to be a paranormal expert. That's upsetting to many. There are people who don't want to think of loved ones stuck and unable to pass on in peace. What if someone he deceived uncovered his ruse and wanted revenge?"

"Do you think it was someone from last night's event who pushed Mr Lombard down the cellar stairs?" Matthew tickled the puppy under his chin.

The dog was an adorable creature. He'd been rescued from a puppy farm the dogs' home I volunteered at uncovered. We'd raced to save the puppies and successfully re-homed all of them. Unfortunately, this one was lame and had a malformed front leg, so no one wanted to take a chance on him.

"You said the cellar door was locked," my mother said. "How could anyone living get through a locked door and push that man down the stairs?"

"Someone could have seen where Joe put the cellar key," I said. "When the lights went out, it was the perfect opportunity to sneak the key off the shelf and murder Mr Lombard."

"I doubt it was his publisher," Matthew said. "He was making money off of the books."

"The ghost trend could be on the decline, so Nicholas got rid of a liability," I said. "However, I'm concerned Inspector Templeton spent a long time speaking to Joe."

"Joe Patterson is a fine landlord," my mother exclaimed. "I've known him for years. When I wasn't bedbound and weakened by a chronic fever, I'd often visit the Craven Arms for a lemonade and a warm by the fire."

"Joe has a colourful past, though, and I don't want Inspector Templeton focused on him, to the detriment of the other suspects." I covered my mouth as I gently coughed.

My mother grabbed the book and flicked through it. "You should stay home today."

"Why would that be?"

"Mr Lombard says here when someone develops a troubling cough, it means a spirit has entered their body. You need an exorcism."

I cast my gaze to the ceiling. "I'll need a stiff gin if you keep up that nonsense."

"You've been around angry spirits." My mother waved a crumpled handkerchief at me as if it would ward off evil. "You could have brought something dangerous home. What if you're carrying the ghost who killed Mr Lombard? It could come for me next."

"Then Inspector Templeton would need to arrest me for your murder, wouldn't he? Although how he'd prove there was a ghost living inside me, I couldn't say." I tugged the handkerchief from my mother's hand, before her frantic waving caused her to pull a muscle.

My mother sniffed. "Go back to bed. Matthew, telephone the parish priest."

I collected my empty bowl and cup and headed to the door. "I have obituaries to write. I have no time to be exercised. Or should that be exorcised? No matter. It's not happening. And at this stage in the investigation, it's too early to know if Mr Lombard's death was an accident or deliberate. There will be an autopsy to determine the cause of death."

"Let's hope it was an accident," my mother said. "We could do without having another murder on our hands. Our business will get a reputation."

I hesitated at the door. "I still can't figure out why he cried out for help just before he fell. We all heard him."

"Mr Lombard scared himself," Matthew said. "He most likely heard a pipe rattle and convinced himself something was chasing him, ran up the stairs, got to the top, and realised his error. He lost his bearings in the dark and fell."

I considered the possibility. "He had been drinking. In the dark, after a few glasses of wine, he simply made a terrible mistake."

"Are you sure I can't convince you to return to your bed?" my mother asked. "Your cough had a gurgling wheeze to it. Mr Lombard says in this book that gurgling noises represent evil spirits. The parish priest could be here in under an hour."

"I'm happy to carry this ghost so long as it does me no harm. I must go to work." I hurried away, being as polite as possible as I ignored my mother's continued remonstrations. She was convinced I'd been affected by a spirit who would throttle me from the inside out as I slowly gurgled my way to a miserable death.

I left her in Matthew's capable hands and hurried out of the front door with Benji to walk the brisk twenty minutes to the London Times office.

I'd barely taken off my coat before Bob Flanders, fellow journalist and royal pain in my behind, appeared.

"I'm not late," I said, in lieu of a greeting.

"You're cutting it fine."

"I'm five minutes early."

Bob ran a hand down his crumpled shirt front. "I get the dead guy."

I brushed past him and headed to my desk. I had the smallest desk in the office with the worst lighting, but it was my own space, and I cherished it.

Unfortunately, Bob followed me. "I know you were there last night, but I get to write this article. I've already checked with Harry, and he said it's my story."

I busied myself with my notepad and pencil, settling Benji beside me. "I'm uncertain why you're talking to me, since you've already made a decision in my absence."

"You write the book review. Don't overstretch and embarrass yourself."

I glanced up at Bob and tapped my pencil against my chin. "And if I choose to argue? After all, an eyewitness account is more valuable than a reporter getting statements and putting his own slant on things. As you correctly uncovered, I was at the crime scene. I saw everything."

Bob rapped his knuckles on my desk and leaned closer. Only a warning growl from Benji kept him a respectable distance away. "Stay away from my story. I've already talked to the police, so I know there's something fishy going on."

"I could refer you back to my last comment, but I fear it didn't go into those weary brain cells the first time. Perhaps I should repeat myself but use words with fewer syllables. You do know what a syllable is, don't you, Bob?"

"Is this your new chap?"

I stiffened in my seat and slowly turned. Isabella Michaels, a reporter working for a tawdry tabloid newspaper, stood behind me, a smirk on her face and her camera slung over one shoulder on a long black strap. "I don't believe we've had the pleasure."

"You're welcome to everything Bob has to offer a woman," I said. "Although he was just off to scrub an egg stain from his tie before he starts work."

Bob looked at his perfectly clean tie and scowled. "Remember, you get the book review. Leave the real reporting to me." He turned and stomped away.

"He's deliciously charmless." Isabella walked over and perched on the edge of my desk. She patted Benji on the head.

"Bob is known for exactly that. Uncle Harry keeps him around because he feels sorry for him." I sighed. "That was mean. He writes a decent story. What are you doing here?"

She smiled brightly at me. "I hear we have a murder."

"We! I don't think so." I turned away.

"Come on, old bean. Don't be like that. We must stick together, especially when there are the likes of Bob and his grubby tie to deal with. He gave you the book review as if he was offering you the crown jewels. The cheek of the man."

I glanced at her. "We've never stuck together before. Why the change of heart?"

Isabella tilted her head from side to side. "I know things about your pub."

"Which one?"

"Don't play coy. The Craven Arms. The ghosts. The murder."

"Since you weren't there last night, I doubt very much you know more than me."

She huffed out a breath. "Why do you have to be so stubborn?"

"It's a handy trait when you're a journalist. You should know that." I paused and studied her. "I'll bite. What do you know?"

Isabella glanced around and leaned closer. "We don't always see eye to eye, but I know you don't judge people."

"I do. Although I try not to let my judgements colour my opinions. And when I'm wrong, I say I am."

"That's what I thought." Isabella hesitated. "I don't want you judging my family when I tell you this, but I have useful information about the ghost hunter who died last night."

She had my full attention. "I'm listening."

Isabella swiped her hair out of her eyes. "If you laugh, we'll be sworn enemies."

"I thought we already were." I pursed my lips when she frowned at me. "Whatever you tell me, I'll take it seriously."

She drew in a breath. "My aunt is a spiritualist. She's well known locally. Before she became housebound with her illness, she performed as Madame Blanc."

Although I wasn't a believer, I was curious to learn more. "And she's had a message from the other side?"

"No! Not from a ghost. William Lombard, the dead chap, he consulted with her."

I blinked at her in wide-eyed surprise. "About what?"

"I wasn't there, but I know he visited her several times."

I leaned back in my seat. "Why are you telling me this?"

"Because, unlike many journalists, you won't make fun of my aunt's beliefs. I haven't even told the police yet because I know how they'd respond." Isabella wrinkled her nose. "I want to do a deal with you."

"What are the terms of this deal?"

"You give me a first-hand account of what happened at the Craven Arms and let me take photographs of the inside of the pub and the cellar, and I'll grant you an exclusive interview with my aunt." Isabella held out a hand for me to shake. "What do you say?"

Chapter 7

I'd barely had to weigh up the options before firmly shaking Isabella's hand. If I could get the scoop on Bob and gather information to help with the investigation, I'd convince Uncle Harry I was the ideal journalist to write the article.

After making the deal, Isabella had left. We'd arranged to meet at lunchtime at her aunt's residence.

I got to work on two obituaries. One for an elderly lady, who'd died peacefully surrounded by family, and the other for a one-armed bus conductor, who'd lost his footing and his grip and fell onto the road, never to get up again.

I stopped by Uncle Harry's office before I left for my meeting with Isabella's aunt. "I know you don't like me interfering in other journalists' stories, but I've got an exclusive tip to follow up. I'll do it during my lunch break."

Uncle Harry grunted. He was engrossed in the latest round of edits. "Which story?"

"The death at the Craven Arms."

His head jerked up. "Veronica, don't make me warn you off. Bob was in early this morning, and I hadn't even had my first cup of coffee before he insisted he run with that story and he was the best man for the job."

"What a cruel thing to do, bother a man before he's caffeinated."

Uncle Harry raised an eyebrow. "I was planning on giving him the story anyway, provided he turns his latest piece in on time, but I could have done without the hassle. He only bothered me because he knew you'd ask for it."

"Bob wants the story because it'll give him an opportunity to go to a pub in a work capacity. I expect he'll charge his drinking expenses to the newspaper."

"He can try." Uncle Harry sat back in his seat. "I know you were there, so make sure Bob gets all the information he needs. Is that where you're headed? Back to the Craven Arms?"

"No. I can say little about my tipoff. But it could be valuable."

"If it is, don't keep the information to yourself. I don't want to get a headache because of Bob's whining."

"Perish the thought." I blew him a kiss, collected my handbag and coat, and left the office with Benji. I checked the address Isabella had given me for her aunt, Maud Baxter. It was a house in a poor part of London and too far to walk to, so I hailed a taxi, and we were there within twenty minutes, the well-kept offices and streets giving way to slum terraces and unmaintained roads.

"Are you sure this is the place, miss?" the cabbie asked as he pulled up outside forty-seven Grey Street.

"Quite sure. Thank you." I handed over the fare.

"I can stay and keep the meter running. I don't like to think of a lady out and about in these parts on her own."

"How thoughtful. But I'm meeting someone. We'll be perfectly safe together. And I have my dog. He's wonderfully protective."

The cabbie didn't look convinced, and watched until I'd reached the door and knocked. Isabella opened it. She ushered us inside and closed the door on a gloomy but tidy hallway. There was a large mirror on one wall and a coat rack on the other.

I noted several pairs of smart heels placed beneath the coats. "I didn't realise you lived here."

Isabella's forehead furrowed. "What makes you say that?"

"Does your aunt have a liking for impractical shoes?" I gestured at the heels.

"Oh! They're mine. This is temporary, though. I've been staying because my aunt's not been well. We're not a big family, and I didn't want her ill and alone."

"How thoughtful." I was aware of Isabella's circumstances. The newspaper she worked at paid poorly and treated its journalists with little respect, especially their female workforce.

There was a squawk from close by, and Benji's ears pricked.

"My aunt has a parrot. She says he's her spirit animal." Isabella rolled her eyes.

"I remember reading an article about certain tribes having spirit animals. I didn't realise it was the same for spiritualists."

"Pay no attention to the bird or any nonsense talk about spirit animals. My aunt is old, and she gets confused. She found the thing half-dead in the park and carried it home. It was probably someone's pet that escaped. She nursed it back to health, and now the thing won't leave her side. Be careful, though, it bites."

Isabella led me and Benji along the small hallway. We passed a smart front parlour, and there was a kitchen at the back. Isabella took us into a room next to the kitchen. There was a round table in the centre with several chairs. A cabinet and sideboard were littered with bottles and candles. An elderly woman with a double chin, a thick mop of wild iron-grey curls, and a slash of red lipstick occupied one of the chairs.

"Auntie, this is the journalist I was telling you about, Veronica Vale."

Aunt Maud held out a ring-encrusted hand. Rather than simply shaking it, she clasped my hand between both of hers and held on tight. "What energy you have, my child. So much vim and vigour."

"That's kind of you to say," I said.

"You spend a lot of time with the dead. Fascinating. Thinking about them, and … something else. You're in the business of helping the dead?"

I indulged her with a smile. "I suspect Isabella has told you about my work as an obituary writer."

"It's not that. It's a feeling I have about you. Sometimes too smart for your own good, too. It can get you into trouble."

"And I'm sure Isabella has told you about my occasional encounters with a certain police inspector who doesn't appreciate me telling him what to do."

"I'm too busy to gossip about you," Isabella muttered. "Take a seat."

Aunt Maud finally released my hand. Her attention turned to Benji. "Isabella, be a good girl and fetch the biscuit tin. There'll be something plain in there to entice this charming fellow. Perhaps a digestive."

"If you give Benji a biscuit, you'll be his friend for life," I said. My attention turned to the splendid red and blue parrot perched on an upright lampstand, chewing a piece of apple.

"That's Horatio," Aunt Maud said, stroking Benji. "My spirit animal. Cleverer than me. Parrots have long memories and are excellent mimics. When treated well, they live as long as humans. I'm certain he'll outlive me. Although, I've heard spirit animals die when the person they're bonded to expires. I hope that's not the case for Horatio."

"He's a beautiful bird," I said.

Aunt Maud's beady eyes glistened. "I can tell you like animals."

"Adore them." I inched closer to the parrot.

"Perhaps you'd like him when the time comes."

I eyed the parrot's giant beak and vicious-looking claws. "I'm no avian expert, but I can ask around to see if there are any willing foster homes."

"The sooner the better. I'm ill and old. If it weren't for Isabella taking pity on me, I'd long be in the ground."

Her words reminded me of how my own mother fretted about her health. I smiled and took a seat. Isabella returned to the room with a tea tray and biscuits. Nothing was said as tea was poured, and Benji was fed a plain digestive, which he thoroughly enjoyed.

"Mind your manners," the parrot said.

"Oh! How delightful. He talks!" I exclaimed.

"Horatio learned everything before he came to me," Aunt Maud said. "And he speaks in tongues. The spirits use him, so don't be alarmed if odd things come out of his beak."

I admired the parrot for another second before extracting my notepad and setting it on the table. Isabella joined us, settling in beside her aunt and giving her hand a gentle squeeze.

"I'd like to ask you about your meetings with William Lombard," I said.

"I don't want to bother with that," Aunt Maud said. "We're here to hold a seance. That way, we can speak directly to William."

"I'm only here for the facts," I said.

"Why talk to me when you can speak directly to him? Isabella, bring out the communication board."

"Aunt, we discussed this." Isabella's tone was firm but gentle. "Veronica needs to know about your meetings with William when he was alive."

"Silly old bird," the parrot said.

Aunt Maud rumbled a laugh. "I'm sorry. I focus on those no longer with us rather than on the living. It does make me a silly old bird."

"I'm not sure what Isabella has told you," I said, "but my family owns the Craven Arms, the pub where Mr Lombard died. I'm gathering information to help the police figure out what happened to him."

"And ensure I have a front-page article with my name on the byline," Isabella said.

"It's long overdue. You're such a talented writer. Did you know Isabella has written a novel?" Aunt Maud asked.

I inclined my head. "We've never discussed novels."

"Veronica isn't interested in my scribblings. She's just here to get information on Mr Lombard." Isabella's cheeks flushed, and she looked away.

"Payment first," Aunt Maud said.

I stared at Isabella, but she shrugged.

"Whenever anyone has a reading, I take payment up front," Aunt Maud said. "Sometimes, people get frightened and run off. If I haven't collected what's owed me, I'm out of pocket. And with my knees, I can't chase after them."

I could have protested, and I should. Isabella made no mention of paying her aunt for information, but a glance around the room showed the carpet was threadbare, and the cups chipped. Neither Isabella nor her aunt lived an extravagant lifestyle. I extracted money and set it on the table. It vanished in the blink of an eye.

"Ask your questions," Aunt Maud said.

"How many times did Mr Lombard visit you?" I asked.

"Isabella, get my diary."

Isabella leaned over to a cluttered cabinet and extracted a thick leather-bound book and passed it to her aunt. She flicked through it for a moment.

"Five meetings over the last year. He first came to see me after his sister died," Aunt Maud said.

"I wasn't aware he'd lost a sister."

She closed the diary. "They weren't close. He hadn't been in touch with her for years."

"He wasn't here to communicate with her spirit and pass on last words?" I asked.

"Nothing so noble. He didn't care about her. But his sister had expensive jewels she'd been given by a former fiancé. She'd hidden them, and William wanted them for himself."

"Goodness! How did you know about her jewels?"

Aunt Maud grunted out a laugh. "Her ghost told me, of course."

"Ghost. Ghost. Ghost!" The parrot squawked and flapped his wings, sending up a flurry of dust and small feathers.

"I've done some research on Mr Lombard," Isabella said. "He hasn't always been a paranormal investigator."

I nodded. "He was a Bible salesman."

"That's right. He started dabbling in the paranormal five years ago. As public interest grew, so did his so-called experience. He began running small tours in supposedly haunted places. That work expanded, and then he got an offer to write a book."

"Mr Lombard must have believed in the paranormal if he consulted you," I said to Aunt Maud.

She shook her head. "He wasn't a believer. I didn't need to hold his hand to realise he had no pure motives. He saw an opportunity to make money, and he took it, using whatever means necessary. He most likely thought I had some ruse going. Connections to get him the information he needed."

I nodded to myself. Last night's ghost hunt had been more theatrical than professional. The flickering lights, strange noises, hammy excitement. And I wasn't convinced the camera Mr Lombard used even worked.

"Did Mr Lombard ever find the jewels?" I asked.

"As far as I know, they're still tucked away," Aunt Maud said. "His sister hasn't been back since his last visit, so she could have passed over now the threat of her brother's greed has gone. Everyone join hands. We'll conduct a seance and talk to William."

I kept my fingers firmly wrapped around my pencil. "Before we do, is there anything else you can tell me about Mr Lombard?"

"He'll tell you everything himself when we make contact." Aunt Maud leaned forward again, plucked the pencil from my grasp, and grabbed my hands. She sucked in a breath. "I'm so sorry."

"What are you sorry for?"

Tears glazed her eyes. "The explosion."

"I don't understand." I looked at Isabella for clarity, but she shook her head.

Aunt Maud slumped back. "I get these flashes. Visions. I don't know where they come from. Your dog can join in."

"Join in?"

"With the seance. Ghosts like animals. They're simple creatures and never have an ulterior motive. You always know where you stand with a dog."

I couldn't argue with that, and I was so bewildered by Aunt Maud's odd comments that I didn't protest as we joined hands, Benji included, to begin the seance.

"This could get strange," Isabella muttered. "Stay in your seat, and everything will be fine."

Before I had an opportunity to ask what kind of strange she referred to, Aunt Maud jerked rigid in her seat, and her eyes widened.

"Should we call for help?" I peered at her.

"This is normal. She's making contact," Isabella whispered. "Give her a minute."

"Crazy bird. Bad bird. Tell the truth," the parrot squawked.

I slid a glance at Isabella. "Do you think this is real?"

"It is! At least to her. Stop talking, or you'll distract her."

I prevented more questions from tumbling out by pressing my lips together, aware my hand was going numb from being gripped so tightly.

The lights flickered and Horatio stopped squawking. Benji whined.

Aunt Maud's eyes bulged, and she groaned. "It was murder! He was poisoned."

Chapter 8

I welcomed the cool breeze against my skin as I stood outside Aunt Maud's small terraced house with Isabella, who smoked a cigarette.

"Are your aunt's seances always that intense?" I asked.

"It depends who she's speaking to," Isabella said. "Some spirits can be mean. Most of them are confused. They get rude because they don't understand what's going on."

I glanced at her to check if she was being sincere or teasing. "Do you really believe all of that?"

Isabella lifted a shoulder. "I've been around Aunt Maud long enough to know she's not faking it. Maybe it's not ghosts communicating with her, but she senses things. And she's predicted the future, so there's something in it." Isabella blew out a plume of smoke.

"What has she predicted?"

"Accidents. Usually, unhappy times to come. She never shares the bad news with her clients, though. What would be the point? Their fate is sealed."

"You make your own fate."

"If you say so."

"Your aunt is excellent at reading people. Or perhaps she has the right connections so she can unearth secrets." I tilted my head. "She could have learned all those things about me from you."

Isabella stubbed out her cigarette. "I already told you that I don't waste time gossiping about you to anyone."

"You have mentioned me to your aunt, though?" I asked.

"Your name may have come up."

"It's not hard to find out information about a person. The library archive is a wonderful resource. Or your aunt could have contacted the newspaper to learn of my credentials."

"My aunt is housebound and sick. She barely has the energy to get out of bed most mornings, let alone winkle out information on her clients."

I stepped back as a group of dirty, scrape-kneed children dashed past. "I saw the bottle of morphine on the sideboard. How long does she have?"

Isabella scowled at me. "That's none of your business."

"We may not be allies, but we share similarities. My mother can be difficult, too. I don't think she's as sick as your aunt, but she never fully recovered from my father's death. She still grieves him, and sometimes it becomes too much for her to bear and she numbs the pain."

Isabella's gaze shifted to the road. "What does that have to do with me?"

"My mother went through a period of using laudanum. She said it helped her to sleep, but she was using it to chase away the sadness. It did her no good. It took time and effort to stop her from using it to excess. The change in the law helped, making it harder to come by."

Isabella fell silent, her fingers fiddling with a loose thread on her jacket hem. "Aunt Maud has cancer. She needs the morphine for her physical pain. The doctor said it helps her to cope."

My heart went out to her. "I'm sure it does."

"How's your mother doing now?" Isabella asked after a moment of silence.

"She spends most of her days in a state of chronic anxiety, worrying about me, Matthew, Benji, or the general state of the world. That can be difficult to live with, but she no longer needs anything to numb her sadness."

Isabella went quiet again. "What is the point of your nosiness? It's a dreadful habit."

"No point. Not really. But I thought you'd get comfort from knowing you're not alone."

"I am! It's me and my aunt. You don't see anyone else helping." Isabella looked along the street and sighed. "I don't mind. Not really. Aunt Maud's been good to me. My old mother was never around when I was growing up. She worked, so I fended for myself the best I could."

"Were you an only child?"

"I had a brother. He died." Isabella pulled out another cigarette but didn't light it. "Aunt Maud's door was always open. She never had two brass farthings to rub together, but she had an endless amount of kindness and hugs, and there was always food for me. Even if it meant she went without. She's a good old thing."

"You said she has a lot of repeat clients," I said. "That must make her a reasonable living."

"Silly goose barely charges for her services," Isabella said. "I told her you were good for it, though. But most people who come here are poor and suffering. She takes a pittance from them. She may not look it, but she's softhearted."

"You'll miss her when she's gone," I said.

Isabella brushed her hands together. "When can I get into the pub for my photographs? I don't want you going back on our deal."

The topic of Aunt Maud's ill health had been closed. "We can stop by this evening. I need to check the police have gone, and the pub is open again, but it should be fine. I'll telephone to confirm the details, but if all is well, we can meet at eight o'clock."

"I want photographs of the cellar. I'm determined to get my name on the front page. When other journalists see what an incredible writer I am and the inside scoop I've snagged, I'll finally get out of there and into a decent job."

I wanted to wish Isabella luck with that endeavour, knowing how difficult it was being a woman in an industry dominated by men, but given the mood she was in, I was certain she'd take offense and snap. And although our truce may be temporary, I didn't want to be the first to lob a grenade and restart the war.

We said our goodbyes, and Isabella returned to the house. I walked to the end of the street with Benji, hailed a taxi, and returned to work. No beggars, troublemakers, or ner' do wells bothered me. Benji was an excellent deterrent to anyone who had a mind for making trouble.

When I got to my desk, I picked up the telephone and called Inspector Templeton. I wanted to see if there was any truth to what Aunt Maud had told me about the poison. It made sense. When I'd seen Mr Lombard's body, there'd been no obvious head injury or blood on the cellar floor. Of course, if he'd fallen and broken his neck, that would have done him in, but poison would have been just as effective.

I was on hold for several minutes before finally being connected to Inspector Templeton. "I was thinking you were avoiding me."

"As tempting as that is, I know you'd seek me out. What is it?"

"You sound stressed."

"My job isn't all afternoon tea and polite conversation. What do you want, Veronica?"

"Goodness! If you're going to be like that, I shan't waste your time."

"Wait! You called for a reason. It's never small talk with you. Is there something you need?" Inspector Templeton asked.

"I'll answer that question if you tell me why you're being so abrupt? I've barely trodden on your toes during this investigation, so it can't be that causing your surly tone."

"So far you haven't. But it's only a matter of time."

"It's nice to hear how much you welcome my assistance."

He remained silent for an uncomfortable length of time before sighing. "There's been an order from up high. There's to be more slum clearance. There have been complaints about the number of homeless men causing problems. Begging, making a nuisance of themselves, that sort of thing."

"If you move them from the slums, where will they go?"

"Apparently, that's not our concern. A team is being put together to ferret them out."

"That's hardly the work of someone who investigates murder."

"It's a huge job, so it's all hands on deck. I've been ordered to take some shifts to show I'm willing. I suppose the extra money will be useful, but it leaves a bad taste in the mouth." He heaved out another sigh.

"Are you saving for something in particular?"

"I'm retiring abroad, where you can't follow me."

I smiled. "Spain is rather lovely. If you retire there, I'll definitely follow you."

"Is that a threat, or a promise?"

"Really, there's no need for that." I drew in a breath. "I called with information about William Lombard's death. But I have a question for you first."

"Go ahead."

"Was he killed using poison?"

Inspector Templeton inhaled sharply. "How the devil did you know that?"

My heart skipped a beat. "Is it true?"

"Veronica! This is serious. That information has not been released to the public. I'm one of the few people who knows. How did you find out? Do you know who poisoned him?"

"Fear not, Inspector. I didn't dose him with poison. Nor do I know who did."

"Then how do you know?"

This was where the conversation could take a sideways tilt. "A spiritualist told me."

There was silence.

"Are you still there?" I asked.

"A... What?"

"You know the type. Enjoy speaking to the dead. Holds seances. They work out of mysteriously dark rooms. This one has a parrot. Her spirit animal, apparently."

"How is that possible?" There was a shuffling sound on the line. "I need this spiritualist's information. She could have poisoned Mr Lombard."

"The woman is housebound and ailing. She's not the person you're looking for."

"Are you certain she wasn't at the Craven Arms on the night of the murder?"

"Absolutely certain. Well, my source can be slippery, but I don't think Isabella would lie about this."

"Isabella? Isabella Michaels? She put you in touch with this spiritualist?"

"Yes, but that's beside the point. Don't focus on the spiritualist. What kind of poison was used to murder Mr Lombard?"

"This is an ongoing investigation."

"Of which I'm fully aware. But if a man was murdered in one of my pubs, surely, I have a right to be kept informed."

"And I have the right to consider you a suspect, since you were there when the death occurred."

"You have my statement. I was with Ruby and Benji. Besides, you know me well enough to comprehend that the list of people I wish to snuff out is small." It ran to barely a dozen names.

"There's a list?" Inspector Templeton sounded startled.

I chuckled. "You're not on it. At least not this month."

"I need to speak to the spiritualist," Inspector Templeton said, all serious tones and no fun at all.

"I doubt she'll be useful. And she'll require payment before she talks."

"Payment! This gets worse. How did she know Mr Lombard?"

"He visited her on a personal matter, but she got to know his character."

"And she claims to have communicated with him when he was a ghost? She told you how he died?"

"If only it was that easy, then you'd have no unsolved cases," I said. "However, the spiritualist sensed the method of murder. She told me it was poison, but there was no more detail attached. And she said something about an explosion, but I think she got the wrong end of the stick. That's all she told me."

"I'll still need her information."

Somewhat reluctantly, I passed on Aunt Maud's details to Inspector Templeton, warning him to handle her carefully since she was unwell and to watch out for Isabella.

"Do you have any more information about the type of poison used?" I was pressing my luck by pushing, but my curiosity remained piqued.

"If I tell you the basics, will you stop pestering me?"

"I make no guarantees."

It sounded like Inspector Templeton growled. "We don't have all the results from the autopsy, but there were no signs of physical injury."

"Mr Lombard's neck wasn't broken?"

"No broken bones, just bruising where he hit the steps on his way down. A blood sample revealed abnormalities."

"The poison?"

"Possibly."

"That means Mr Lombard fell because he was unwell," I said. "Before he went into the cellar, he was sweating and flexing his fingers. Was that because the poison was already affecting him?"

"I can't yet confirm that. Again, it's possible."

"If it was a slow-acting poison, it could have hampered his reflexes or caused pain. Mr Lombard wouldn't have known what was going on, so would have carried on as usual." My gaze swept around the busy office. "I assumed he was sweating from the stress of fabricating ghosts, although he seemed in good spirits when he was reading from his book. Depending on what poison was used, it could even have been administered earlier in the day, before he arrived at the Craven Arms. Do you know all of his movements from that day?"

"We're investigating all angles," Inspector Templeton said.

"And they are?"

"Something you don't need to know."

Despite asking the same question in several ways, he furnished me with no further information. Frustrating man.

"I'm assuming it's safe to reopen the Craven Arms? You've collected all the evidence you need?" I asked.

"It's already open." Inspector Templeton shuffled some papers, making the line sound crackly. "And I won't bother telling you to keep out of this, since the pub is a going concern of yours."

"Excellent. I prefer it when we work together."

"You don't ever give me much choice."

I held in a laugh. We said our goodbyes, and I set the telephone in its cradle. I always appreciated when a man showed common sense.

The rest of the day, I was focused on writing obituaries. There was a fascinating death involving a milk float, several crates of full-fat milk, and a misbehaving cat. It wasn't the cat that met a fateful end, but the unlucky milkman who chased it when it drank from a pint of milk, and toppled the crates. The milkman was struck by a car and didn't get up again.

As my working day drew to an end, I contacted Ruby and Isabella to let them know we'd be meeting at the Craven Arms, then tidied my desk, grabbed a bite to eat with Benji in the local cafe, and hopped in a taxi to go back to the scene of the crime.

I was the first to arrive and found the pub quiet. Joe looked bored as he stood behind the bar polishing glasses.

He smiled when he saw me. "I figured you'd be back to see how much of a mess the coppers made. Same as usual?"

"Yes, please. It's been a long day." I looked around at the half a dozen customers. "Is it usually this quiet?"

"There's a big football match on tonight. Delayed from last month because of pitch flooding, so they squeezed it in this evening. The place will be bursting at the seams once the full-time whistle blows."

I thanked him for my drink when he delivered it. "Were the police much of a bother?"

"They were good enough. They always unsettle me, but other than asking lots of questions, they kept out of my way, and I kept out of theirs. I was happy when they moved the body out of the cellar."

"The investigation is moving quickly. They'll soon figure out what happened to Mr Lombard."

The pub door opened, and Isabella strode in with a camera tucked under her arm. She lifted a hand in greeting and walked over. I made the introductions, but Isabella refused the offer of a drink, preferring to take photographs, so Joe took her to get to work.

I sat at the bar and sipped my gin fizz, relaxing in the low murmur of conversation and inhaling the all-too familiar scent of ale and old wood. These were the scents of my childhood.

Ruby blasted through the door a few moments later, throwing out apologies as she smoothed her hair. "I've had a horror of a day. And I'm so stiff."

"Too much riding?" I asked.

"Must be that. Lady M has three new horses, and none of them have been properly trained. I was thrown off twice. It's fortunate I know how to land safely." She rolled her shoulders and winced. "The landings weren't perfect, though. I'll have a bruise on my backside the size of Wales!"

"I didn't have time to tell you on the telephone earlier today, but I learned Mr Lombard was poisoned," I muttered, being certain no one else could overhear.

Ruby's eyes widened. "Poisoned when he was here?"

"It's possible."

"There was food and drink laid on," Ruby said. "Something in that?"

"We all ate the food," I said. "Joe, could you help us with something?"

"Anything for you." He walked over and joined us.

"Have you had reports from customers saying they felt unwell after the book reading and ghost hunt?" I asked.

He shook his head. "Nothing's gotten back to me. Why do you ask?"

"We're concerned there was something wrong with the food. Where did you get it from?"

"Our usual lady. Mrs Simpson on Wheatfield Street. She's provided the food for twenty years. Has a way with the nibbles and sandwiches people like, so I always use her. Decent rates, too. She'd never make anything with spoiled meat."

"It was just finger food," Ruby said. "Nothing rich."

"Could it have been the fish paste?" Joe asked.

"Benji had a fish paste sandwich, and he's fine," I said.

Benji wagged his tail to confirm he was in the best of health.

"I'll confess to sneaking a couple of sandwiches myself. And I feel fine. You don't think that's what did Mr Lombard in, do you?" Joe asked.

"We're looking at all possibilities," I said.

"Am I allowed into the cellar?" Isabella called out as she lowered her camera.

"Be careful." Joe pointed at the cellar door. "It's unlocked, but the steps are uneven. I don't want any more accidents."

Isabella opened the door and slipped out of sight.

"Are you two best friends now?" There was a hint of jealousy in Ruby's tone.

"That'll never happen. But she provided me with useful information, so I'm doing her a favour. She wants her article on the front page of the newspaper."

"I wish her the best of luck," Ruby said. "Joe, check the wine racks after Isabella returns. Make sure she doesn't sneak anything into her handbag."

Joe chuckled. "Will do."

"You didn't have a problem with Mr Lombard, did you?" I asked.

"Didn't know the fella. And I didn't stay for the ghost nonsense. I was in the back room with my feet up, listening to the radio."

"I thought as much. You didn't see him fight with anyone that evening?"

"Can't say I did. But it was a busy night."

"It was a hectic evening," I said.

"So hectic someone could easily have slipped poison into Mr Lombard's food," Ruby said. "Maybe that's why he was the only one who got sick."

Joe reared back. "Poison! Nobody said anything about poison."

The pub door opened again, and I was surprised to see Inspector Templeton. If he was surprised to see me, he didn't show it as he walked to the bar.

"Back so soon?" Joe still looked flustered by Ruby's poison proclamation. "I'm assuming this isn't a social visit."

"You assume right." Inspector Templeton nodded at me and Ruby. "Joe, we need to talk about your fight with William Lombard."

Chapter 9

I stared in astonishment at Inspector Templeton. "What fight? Joe didn't know the man."

Isabella appeared from out of the cellar, her eyes gleaming with interest as she saw Inspector Templeton by the bar. She hurried over to join us.

"Feel free to take more photographs on the other side of the pub," I said. "The fireplace is a particularly lovely feature."

"I'm perfect right here. And I sense a story in the making." Isabella grinned salaciously.

I chose to ignore her. "What's the meaning of your visit?" I asked Inspector Templeton. "We should take this somewhere quieter." Inspector Templeton addressed Joe. "Where there'll be less interference."

"Veronica can hear anything we talk about," Joe said. "I hide nothing from her. She's a fair boss. Just like her old dad."

"And Joe is an upstanding citizen," I said. "He didn't know Mr Lombard, so has nothing to do with recent events."

"If that's true, then why do I have eyewitness statements claiming there was a dispute between Joe and Mr Lombard on the day of his death?" Inspector Templeton asked.

"The eyewitnesses are wrong," I said. "Just a few moments ago, I confirmed with Joe that he didn't know Mr Lombard. He'd hardly squabble with a stranger, would he?"

Joe refused to meet my gaze and returned to polishing his already clean pint glasses.

"What did you argue about?" Isabella had her notepad out and pencil poised.

"Don't print lies in your tattle rag," I said. "You're only here to take photographs."

"I'm not missing an opportunity like this. You knew Mr Lombard? Or should I say, the victim?" she asked Joe.

"Victim? I... I didn't! I mean, I knew of him because his publisher had been in touch. I wasn't keen. I didn't want this place getting a reputation and having odd types, expecting to talk to ghosts over a pint and a packet of peanuts."

"Are you telling me there was a dispute?" I asked.

"A dispute that led to you killing Mr Lombard?" Isabella asked.

"If you have nothing intelligent to say, keep your mouth closed," I said sternly. "I know Joe, and I trust him. He's no killer. He's one of my most hard-working landlords."

"With an extensive criminal record," Inspector Templeton said. "We've been reviewing details and background information on everyone who was at the Craven Arms that night. Joe has a violent past."

"The pertinent word in that sentence being *past*," I said. "Joe didn't hide his history from me or my father. He admitted he had a rough start in life. But people change. Especially if given a second chance and an opportunity to prove themselves without anyone judging their former actions."

"You don't do that with me," Isabella muttered.

"There are exceptions to every rule," I said. "Joe had no reason to argue with Mr Lombard."

"My eyewitnesses are lying?" Inspector Templeton asked.

"I didn't say that, but they're mistaken. Give me their names, and I'll speak to them."

"I'll decline that generous offer," he said. "Joe, answer me truthfully. Did you argue with Mr Lombard?"

Joe pressed his lips together and looked at me. I nodded at him.

His shoulders slumped, and he set down the glass he'd been polishing. "I had a good reason. The deal made was for one evening for a book reading and then a poke about in the dark to look for ghosts."

"Mr Lombard wanted to change the arrangements?" I asked.

"He said the payment had been so generous, they wanted another night for free. I told him to go jump off a bridge. The deal was done, and it wasn't to be changed."

"What did he think about that?" I asked, ignoring Inspector Templeton's irritated look.

"He got mean. Silly fella tried to scare me and said he'd set his ghosts on me. As if I believe in such claptrap. It was all I could do not to laugh in his face."

"How did the disagreement end?" I asked.

"Same as it always does with types that are hot air and no action. He said I'd be hearing from his publisher and I'd be out of a job when you learned what was going on. Apparently, ghosts are money makers." Joe shook his head. "That's when I knew nothing would come of it. I sent him on his way, and he didn't like it, but I won't have Veronica taken advantage of."

"I appreciate your protective stance," I said. "But why lie about having a disagreement with Mr Lombard?"

Joe thrust out his hands. "Because I knew this would happen! The second the police poked around, they'd discover my past and assume the worst. Everyone who knows me now sees I've turned over a new leaf. I'm respectable. I work hard. I give to the poor, and I've even given up the dog fights after Veronica took me to her charity and I adopted one-eyed Billy, god rest his soul."

"He was a wonderful dog. When the time comes, we'll find you a new companion," I said. "A sociable dog who enjoys pub life."

Joe teared up, and he sniffed. "I'd like that. Your family gave me a second chance when no one else would. I'd never be so stupid as to repay that kindness by killing someone."

"In case you're lying," Isabella said, "may I get a photograph of you behind the bar looking menacing?"

"No, you may not." I stood in front of Joe to block Isabella's view. "And unless you want me to test the durability of that camera, you'll stop shoving it in people's faces."

"I'm doing my job, the same as you," Isabella said.

"You're looking for a sensational angle, and that's not acceptable," I said. "You obtained the photographs you wanted. Now it's time for you to go."

Isabella glowered at me for several seconds. "I still want a direct quote from you. And make it sound like the ghost evening scared you."

"You can make up whatever drivel you desire for your newspaper," I said. "I'll give you facts and the facts alone."

Isabella took one more look around, frowning at anyone who caught her eye, then left the pub.

Once that interference was out of the way, Inspector Templeton returned his attention to Joe. "What were you doing during the ghost hunt?"

"I was out the back. I have a room where I take my meals. It had been a long day, and we'd had a delivery come in which I'd had to haul to the cellar on my own. I almost put my back out. When the ghost hunt began, I took a break. I put my feet up and listened to the radio."

"What did you listen to?"

Joe opened his mouth, then snapped it shut. "I forget. It couldn't have been that good. I might have dozed off."

"Which means you have no alibi," Inspector Templeton said.

"Alibi! Why would I need one of those?" Joe looked at me with alarm in his eyes.

"Tell him," I said to Inspector Templeton. "I've not kept things a secret."

A notch furrowed in Inspector Templeton's brow. "I don't discuss investigations with members of the public."

"I was talking to Veronica about dodgy fish paste sandwiches. Is that what you mean?" Joe's gaze flashed from me to Inspector Templeton. "I didn't make them. Oh! And Miss Ruby mentioned poison. It can't be that, though."

"It's true. Poison was involved. We were asking about the food because somebody poisoned Mr Lombard," I said.

"Veronica! Don't share confidential information," Inspector Templeton snapped.

"We all know Joe is innocent!"

"He has a violent past and no alibi for the time of the murder," Inspector Templeton said.

"Wait! Wait!" Joe took a step back, his expression anxious. "I don't want nothing to do with no murder."

"You're innocent," I said. "Inspector Templeton is taking a journey along one of his false avenues of investigation. The more you get to know him, the more common it becomes. But it never gets any less tiresome."

Inspector Templeton glowered at me. "Everyone who attended the book reading has been questioned and ruled out. That leaves our focus on those who remained for the ghost hunt."

"Gosh, this is exciting," Ruby said. "That means I'm a murder suspect, too."

"Having checked your statement alongside Veronica's, I've ruled you out," Inspector Templeton said. "Although perhaps I should find a reason to put you both behind bars to stop you from interfering."

"That's not polite," Ruby said. "Perhaps you'd like a drink, Inspector. You seem stressed."

"He is stressed," I whispered. "Slum clearance duty again."

"Oh no, you poor thing. I don't know how you manage it." Ruby gestured at the bar. "A brandy will set you right."

"Let's focus on the case in hand," Inspector Templeton said. "Joe, I need you to come to the station for questioning."

"That will be a waste of time," I said. "Direct your efforts elsewhere."

"For now, I'm focused on Joe," Inspector Templeton said. "And please, stop telling me how to do my job, or I will arrest you for obstructing justice."

"I'm telling you not to make a fool of yourself. I was just discussing with Joe and Ruby how the poison could have been administered. We can be useful."

"If it was poison, that shows I'm innocent," Joe said. "I'd never use poison to murder."

"Exactly! Joe is fists and violence, not poison. Poison is a delicate mode of murder," I said.

Joe's neck flushed red. "Not that I beat up people anymore, but I take your meaning."

I patted Joe's solid bicep.

"You could have used poison to confuse the situation," Inspector Templeton said. "That's for my team to investigate. Make this easy on yourself and come to the station."

Joe shook his head. "I can't leave the pub. I'll lose trade."

"Must it be now?" I asked.

Inspector Templeton pressed his fingers to his forehead. "As you said yourself, if Joe is innocent, the sooner we rule him out, the sooner we can focus on other suspects."

"I can't shut! I lost the lunchtime trade because your men took so long," Joe said.

"If Inspector Templeton is determined to dig his heels in and question you now, I can look after things until you get back," I said. "Ruby will help."

Ruby fanned her face with a hand. "I know how to pull a pint."

"Then it's all arranged." Inspector Templeton gestured at the door.

"I'm telling you, I'm innocent. And the match day lot will be here soon." Joe flipped the white cloth he'd been using to polish the glasses off his shoulder and dropped it on the bar.

"The questions won't take long, and you'll be back before the end of the match," Inspector Templeton said.

"I'd better be. You don't want these ladies on their own when that crowd rolls up, especially if the home team loses. They can get nasty."

"There are extra patrols on the streets," Inspector Templeton said. "Veronica and Ruby will be safe."

"You don't mind, do you?" I whispered to Ruby. "There's barely anyone in here, so we'll have no trouble keeping an eye on things. It could even be fun. I'll mix you a dry martini with extra olives."

Ruby blinked at me with large, glassy eyes. She didn't answer.

"Come on, old thing. It'll be an hour at most. Isn't that right, Inspector?"

Inspector Templeton nodded. "Providing Joe cooperates."

Ruby hiccupped.

"Steady on. Your drink wasn't that strong, was it?" I asked.

Ruby stood, gripping my arms for support. "I don't feel too chipper." She collapsed to the floor.

Chapter 10

I looked up as a doctor approached along the hospital corridor, hoping for good news. He strode straight past, focused on the clipboard in his hand, scribbling notes and muttering to himself. Todd Smythe, Ruby's younger brother, sat beside me, his hands clasped and his head down.

"We'll hear something any second," I said. "Ruby seemed fine until she fainted."

"She always puts on a brave face." Todd's usually cheerful demeanour was grim and his skin grey with the stress of the situation.

I'd contacted him when we'd been unable to rouse Ruby after she fainted. He'd met us at the local hospital, where we'd been for several hours while Ruby was looked after.

"She's not that brave," I said. "She complains if she gets a blister because her heels rub."

Todd's smile briefly flashed into existence before vanishing. "Do you really think she was poisoned?"

"We won't know for sure until the experts have thoroughly examined her." My words rushed out, and I took a calming breath to settle my panic. "But she was clammy and complaining about muscle stiffness. When she was unconscious, one of her hands was twitching. The chap who died at the Craven Arms had similar symptoms."

"Ruby can't go the same way as your ghost hunter chap." Todd's words caught at the back of his throat.

I placed a reassuring hand on his arm. "Ruby is made of stern stuff. She's been through far worse than a mild case of poisoning, and bounced right back."

Todd didn't seem convinced. "I know the two of you got up to all sorts during the war. Things you can't talk about. But I'll always want to protect her."

"As all brothers should their sisters," I said. "And you're right, Ruby worked tirelessly during the Great War and helped many soldiers and civilians. She got herself out of numerous pickles unscathed. This won't be the last pickle she finds herself in."

Todd stared at the wall, his expression stern. "Our parents are too lenient. She shouldn't get herself into these muddles."

"Ruby didn't deliberately poison herself!"

He dropped his chin to his chest. "I know! Is this my fault? Should I have stopped her from dashing about and getting into trouble?"

"Ruby would never allow that. And if you forced her into a life of tedium, she'd despise you. Ruby is a free spirit. Just like you."

Todd fell silent. "I should contact our parents."

"When Ruby woke briefly, she forbade any of us from contacting your family. And she told you not to make a fuss. You know how cross she'll be if you ignore her."

"She always says that. Never likes anyone to fuss. I should!" He looked away, but not before I noticed the tears in his eyes.

"Chin up. Before you know it, Ruby will be flirting with the doctor and demanding a bouquet to aid in her recovery. I expect she'll want chocolates, too."

Todd forced another smile. "You're right. You know her best out of us. You're as close as sisters. I'll wait until we hear from the doctor before making a telephone call and panicking the rest of the family."

"Sensible advice. There's no need for any of us to fret." I went to pat Benji for reassurance, but the space beside me was empty. Of course, I'd been unable to bring him to the hospital and had left him at the Craven Arms, being looked after by Joe. I missed my dog.

And as much as I reassured Todd not to panic, there was a dreadful swell of unpleasant feeling inside me. If Mr Lombard was poisoned by something he ate or drank at the ghost hunt, it was likely Ruby had been poisoned by the same thing. What if there was no antidote?

As the panicky feeling hit a new note of unpleasantness, Inspector Templeton appeared at the end of the corridor and strode towards us.

"Any news?" I asked him, glad of the distraction.

"I managed a quick word with the doctor overseeing Ruby's recovery." His expression was unreadable. "She's on the mend. They've administered an emetic and tannic acid, followed by a dose of charcoal to eliminate the poison. She'll feel terrible and will need rest, but they're hopeful we got her here in time."

Todd jumped up and embraced Inspector Templeton, slapping him several times on the back. "I can't thank you enough. Veronica said you broke every speed limit to get Ruby here in time."

"It's a privilege of the job. And when I realised Ruby was in trouble, I was happy to help." Inspector Templeton accepted the hug civilly enough.

I searched for something in my handbag, taking a moment to compose myself and blink away tears. Inspector Templeton had been marvellous when Ruby fainted. He'd checked her vital signs, then scooped her into his arms and sprinted to his vehicle, leaving all thoughts of questioning Joe about the murder behind.

I'd sat in the back of the car with Ruby's head cradled on my lap, as Inspector Templeton tore through the streets, turning the air blue with shocking curses as he pushed his vehicle to the limits to ensure we got to the hospital without delay.

It was the action of a hero, and I'd be forever grateful to him.

"This calls for a celebration." Todd stepped back and wiped his eyes. "When can we see Ruby?"

"The doctor said soon. She's resting after purging. It was done more as a precaution than anything else. They'll be out shortly to tell you when you can visit her."

"I'll rustle up tea while we wait." Todd firmly shook Inspector Templeton's hand and then dashed away, a spring in his step.

Inspector Templeton sat beside me. He said nothing, simply rested his hand atop mine for a moment.

Tears welled, but I made a determined effort to remain calm as I cleared my throat. "Thank you. Ruby is so dear to me. I'd be lost without her."

"I know. You're always together, making my life complicated."

"You adore complications," I said. "Your life would be beige without us in it, cajoling you to action and making you see things differently."

"Sometimes, a little beige isn't a bad thing." He patted my hand. "But you're right, you ladies keep me on my toes. I would grieve too if anything bad happened to Ruby."

I looked at him, and the soft, defenseless expression on his face made my heart flip-flop. "What took you so long at the station?"

"I had to fill in an incident report. And while I was there, I chivvied for the results of Mr Lombard's autopsy. I hoped the information would help the doctor treating Ruby."

"Did you discover what poisoned him?"

"Strychnine. And the symptoms fit perfectly."

"What's this?" Todd returned with a tray holding cups of stewed tea and handed them around.

"Strychnine poisoned Mr Lombard," I said.

Inspector Templeton showed no signs of his usual irritation at me sharing the information. "If Mr Lombard was poisoned at the Craven Arms, then it's likely Ruby ingested the same poison. Strychnine poisoning causes muscle stiffness and twitching. It's not a pleasant way to die."

Todd gulped, his cup halfway to his lips. "Ruby won't die, though, will she?"

"No. She must have had a much lower dose than Mr Lombard. And because she's young, strong, and fit, and received swift medical attention, she'll recover," Inspector Templeton said.

Todd shook his head, bewildered. "Who'd want Ruby dead?"

"No one. Ruby wasn't the target," I said. "The poisoner got their man."

"And my sister got in the way and got a stomach full of poison. Poor old thing. Did anyone else become unwell?" Todd asked.

"No one else who attended the ghost hunt has exhibited symptoms of strychnine poisoning," Inspector Templeton said

"Which means it was only Mr Lombard and Ruby who consumed something that night containing strychnine," I said. "I don't recall what Ruby ate, but she always drinks dry martinis. Joe makes them especially for her, so the poison wouldn't have been in her drink."

"Once Ruby is up to having visitors, I'll get a list of everything she consumed," Inspector Templeton said. "That will help us hone in on where the poison was placed. It could also help us figure out who put it there."

We drank tea and waited another half an hour before a doctor approached.

Todd stood and shook his hand. "How is my sister?"

"Miss Smythe is remarkably resilient," he said. "She's awake, sitting up, and talking to everybody. She told us all about the ghost hunt."

"That's excellent news," Todd said. "How long will she have to stay in the hospital?"

The doctor inspected his clipboard. "If she continues to improve, she'll be able to go home tomorrow. But she will need to rest and have someone checking on her. And only plain food for seventy-two hours."

"She could stay in the family home," Todd said a little dubiously. "Although I'm not much of a nursemaid, and our parents are away again. Her old room is dusty, but I can fix it up."

"Don't put yourself out. Ruby is welcome to stay with me," I said. "I insist upon it. She'll be thoroughly pampered, and I'll have someone keep an eye on her at all times. My mother and Matthew are always home."

"That's acceptable," the doctor said. "But if Miss Smythe exhibits any symptoms of distress or if the muscle spasms come back, she must contact her doctor or return to the hospital. She'll feel fragile for a few days, but will make a full recovery."

"Can we see her?" Todd asked.

"It's long past our usual visiting hours," the doctor said, "but you can have five minutes. No more." He directed us to Ruby's room, and then left. It was a small space, but she was in there on her own, and as the doctor described, she was sitting up and fussing with her hair.

"There you all are! And Inspector Templeton is here, too! What a treat," Ruby said. "I thought I'd been abandoned. Veronica, help me. There's an extremely handsome doctor on the ward, and I need to look my best for him."

"Considering you've been poisoned, you look marvellous." I kissed her cheek, thrilled to see my best friend looking so well. "How do you feel?"

"My stomach is growling. I'm unsure if it's the aftereffects of poison or hunger. The doctor did all sorts of unladylike things to me to ensure there was nothing left in my system." She held out her hands. "No more shaking, though. And the muscle stiffness has almost gone. Can you believe it? I was poisoned, too."

"That'll teach you to eat something you shouldn't. Such a greedy old thing." Todd hugged Ruby, then inspected the medical chart at the end of the bed and sidled around the room, back to his old self, now he'd seen his sister was on the road to recovery.

"I can't think what it was. I barely ate a thing that night," Ruby said.

"When you've had a night to rest, I'd like to talk about exactly what you consumed that evening," Inspector Templeton said.

"Of course. I'm happy to help. I could hold a vital clue as to what happened to Mr Lombard," Ruby said.

"Thanks to Inspector Templeton's diligence, we now know what poison was used," I said. "Someone used strychnine on Mr Lombard."

"I'm not familiar with that," Ruby said.

"The doctor believes you only had a small dose," Inspector Templeton said. "And you have youth and good health on your side, which ensured the dose wasn't fatal."

Ruby batted her eyelashes. "That sounded like a compliment, Inspector Templeton.".

"It was. I'm glad you're feeling better." He looked at me. "Do you need a ride home?"

"Yes, please, but I'd like a few more minutes with Ruby."

"I'll wait outside." Inspector Templeton nodded at Ruby, then left the room.

"You gave us all a fright." Todd approached the bed. "When I got the telephone call to say you'd collapsed and were at death's door, I didn't know what to do with myself."

"I was hardly that!" Ruby continued to fuss with her hair, and directed me to tidy it. "But I felt wretched before fainting. I thought I was coming down with a stomach bug. And I got thrown off a horse, so believed my aches and pains were because of a hard landing. I didn't connect the symptoms to anything other than a series of unfortunate events. Did Mr Lombard complain of those symptoms before he died?"

I did my best with Ruby's hair, then stood back from the bed. "If he'd had a big dose of strychnine, the effects would have come on quickly. And once he was locked in the cellar in the dark, he would have been suffering but was unable to do anything about it."

"He must have dragged himself to the top of the stairs and cried out for help but then fainted, like I did."

"What a horrible way to go," Todd said.

"I'm glad I didn't suffer the same fate." Ruby's smile faded.

"Thanks to Inspector Templeton and his quick thinking," I said. "He realised there was something seriously wrong with you and wasted no time in bringing you here."

"I hope you appropriately thanked him on my behalf." Ruby's smile returned.

"I did. He knows how much I appreciate him."

A nurse looked into the room and frowned. "Visiting hours are over. I must ask you to leave. You can come back tomorrow morning."

"As much as I adore seeing you, I could do with some sleep. Although the doctor didn't tell me when I'm getting out. Do either of you know?" Ruby was already snuggling under the crisp white sheets.

"If you have a good night's rest, you can leave tomorrow," I said. "And you're staying with me. It's all been arranged. I'll get a room ready for you and your favourite food in. You'll want for nothing."

Ruby yawned. "Marvellous. We can have midnight feasts like we did when we were children."

We whispered our goodbyes and crept out of the room, easing the door shut.

Todd blew out a relieved breath, the colour returned to his cheeks, and the tension was gone from his shoulders.

I smiled at him as we walked along the corridor. "I'm as relieved as you."

"I'm happy Ruby's on the mend, but I'm angry with whoever did this," Todd said. "If I catch him, I'll give him a thrashing."

"Fear not. Now we know there was a poisoner at the Craven Arms, I'll unmask them. Nothing and nobody will stop me from getting justice for our beloved Ruby."

Chapter 11

I said goodbye to Todd, and he strode off to catch a late-night bus to take him home. Inspector Templeton was waiting for me outside the main doors of the hospital.

It wasn't until we were walking to his vehicle that the exhaustion hit, and I staggered. My best friend had almost died. It was unthinkable. More of those wretched tears appeared, and I failed to blink them away before they fell.

Inspector Templeton put an arm around my waist. "This way. It's not far."

"I need no assistance." I did my best not to sag against him.

"Everybody needs a little assistance now and again. Even the great Veronica Vale when her sturdy nature has taken a battering."

"You make me sound like an elephant."

"Elephants are intelligent creatures. I imagine they can be stubborn too when they desire something."

Under normal circumstances, I'd have protested more, but I barely had the energy to put one foot in front of the other. "I know it's late and an inconvenience, but could we stop by the Craven Arms on the way home?"

"I had already planned that diversion. I assume Benji is missing you."

"And I him. Thank you. I know to most people he's just a dog, but he's one of my closest friends."

"You don't have to explain that to me." Inspector Templeton opened the passenger door for me, and I slid gratefully onto the seat and closed my eyes for a few seconds. He settled in his seat and started the engine, before pulling away from the hospital and onto the almost deserted street.

I was surprised my watch read almost one o'clock in the morning. We'd been at the hospital for five hours. We drove to the Craven Arms in silence. It wasn't the usual spiky silence that often accompanied our journeys. I was deep in thought, and I suspected Inspector Templeton was too.

He pulled up outside the pub. "Do you want me to go in and get Benji?"

"No, I'll do it. Joe will want to know how Ruby's doing. He's ever so fond of her." I climbed out, and after knocking on the locked front door for a moment, Joe appeared. He was still dressed and clearly hadn't gone to bed. Benji was beside him, and he sprang out of the door the second he saw me, wagging his tail.

I crouched and gave him a thorough pat, burying my face into his soft, warm fur.

"I haven't been able to rest since Ruby collapsed," Joe said. "Tell me it's good news."

"It's the best news. The doctor figured out what was wrong with her and she'll make a full recovery."

Joe blew out a breath and clapped his hands together. "I'm so pleased."

"The bad news is, Ruby was poisoned," I said. "Whoever poisoned Mr Lombard accidentally poisoned her, too."

"Those bleeding beggars." Joe scowled. "When I find out who they are, I'll wring their necks. Poisoning a nice lady like Ruby. It's unthinkable."

"I suspect it was an accident, and she wasn't the intended target."

Joe's gaze went over my head to Inspector Templeton. "Not got yourself in trouble with the old bill, have you?"

"No. Inspector Templeton has been helpful. He's taking me home."

"I can drive you if you want. You'll have to ride in my sidecar, but it's comfortable."

"You get to bed. You've had quite enough excitement for one evening." We said our goodbyes, and I left the pub with Benji glued to my leg. This time, I climbed into the back seat so I could sit with Benji and cuddle him.

Inspector Templeton pulled away, and we continued our quiet journey.

"You've been very good about all of this," I said.

"How else would you expect me to be?" Inspector Templeton asked.

"You usually reprimand or scold me."

"These are unusual circumstances. Ruby is your best friend, so I'd expect you to behave exactly this way. And I also expect you to attack this case with renewed vigour given what's happened."

"That's exactly what I intend to do. Even when you complain and threaten to lock me up, so I stop getting in your way."

Inspector Templeton chuckled softly. "I'd expect nothing less from you. Ruby couldn't ask for a better best friend."

I was surprised by his thoughtful words. When we weren't bickering, we had a wonderful partnership.

"Since your thoughts are focused on murder, who do you think did it?" Inspector Templeton asked.

"You really want my input?"

"You'd give it to me, whether I wanted it or not."

"True enough." I settled in the seat, stroking Benji softly. "I should start with the obvious names to get them out of the way. Me and Ruby."

"You were never suspects."

"I'm glad you were thorough enough to consider us, though," I said.

"Ruby's illness sidetracked me from questioning Joe," Inspector Templeton said.

"It wasn't him. You should have heard him when I told him Ruby had been poisoned. He made all sorts of threats."

"That could be a clever cover."

"Joe is a straight-talking man. Uncomplicated."

"He has no alibi. He couldn't remember what show he was listening to on the radio."

"Because you startled him. Panic makes people forget. Ask Joe again, under less stressful circumstances, and he'll come up with the right answer. And yes, he may have bickered with Mr Lombard, but that was because he got greedy. Joe did it to protect me. He doesn't like to think of anyone taking advantage of me."

"He still has a violent past."

I sighed, tiredness making my bones ache. "Question him if you must, but keep an open mind. Joe isn't your man, and there are better suspects."

"Who would you look at as the prime suspect?"

"It must have been another member of the ghost hunt," I said. "I think little of Mr Lombard's publisher, Nicholas Hawthorn. A man obsessed with making endless amounts of money. He was even talking about being able to sell more of Mr Lombard's books now he's dead! What an odious thought. Filling his pockets with coin because somebody died."

"He's a possibility. Who else?"

"There's George Cloister. He's thirsty for fame. And he was quick to offer his services as Mr Lombard's replacement. Perhaps he saw an opportunity too good to miss. Kill the competition and get himself promoted."

"Anyone else?"

"Millicent Baines, of course. She wanted to stop the ghost hunt to prevent her great-grandmother's memory being besmirched. And she snuck back into the Craven Arms. Joe felt sorry for her when she turned on the waterworks, and let her in through the back entrance."

"Do you think Millicent snuck in to murder Mr Lombard?" Inspector Templeton asked.

"She was very angry," I said. "It's possible she did it."

"I had a conversation with Reverend Worthington."

"Of course! I was surprised to see him at the event. Did he have anything useful to add to your investigation?"

"He mentioned seeing a woman hand over a bottle of wine to Joe. Do you know anything about that?"

I lurched forward in my seat. "Grace! I introduced myself to her. She wanted to give Mr Lombard an expensive bottle of wine. Joe commented on the rare vintage. Wine is a perfect vessel for poison."

"That would work. You could inject poison through the cork without anyone noticing it had been tampered with."

I looked over my shoulder. "Turn around. We'll return to the Craven Arms. You can collect the bottle and run tests for strychnine."

"*We* aren't going anywhere."

My heart hammered with excitement. "Inspector! We've identified the delivery method. You must go back."

"I'll send someone to the Craven Arms as soon as I've dropped you and Benji home."

I opened my mouth to protest, but another wave of exhaustion washed over me. I was fagged. "That would work. Joe doesn't deal with the empties until the morning. But be sure to get the right bottle. Joe will tell you what type of wine it was. We don't stock anything that expensive, so it will be easy to find." I settled my hands on my lap. "Have we just discovered our killer?"

"Don't get ahead of yourself. Grace will be questioned, and the evidence collected before we jump to conclusions."

My forehead crinkled. "Why would one of Mr Lombard's fans poison him? Grace was excited to be there."

"Perhaps she realised he was a charlatan, and she'd wasted money and time looking for something that doesn't exist."

I smiled. "Such a cynic."

"You would say the same thing."

"I do."

"I've been in this business long enough to know the world is full of charlatans. They see a weakness and exploit it. Ghost hunting is no different."

I nodded. "Mr Lombard preyed upon those desperate for a word from the other side. He took people's money and sold them dreams. I wonder what dream he sold Grace?"

"In the morning, we'll find out. But right now, you're going home and straight to bed."

If I'd had the energy to bicker, I'd have flung back a barbed comment. But instead, I closed my eyes and sighed. For once, Inspector Templeton was right.

Despite the late hour of my return home, I was up early, washed, dressed, and had grabbed the fastest breakfast of my life before leaving the house. I'd been up so early, I'd even escaped my mother's questioning. And Matthew, as usual, was nowhere to be seen, so it was easy to slip out and return to the hospital.

"Did you bring my makeup?" Ruby asked the second she saw me.

"You didn't request makeup. You look well."

"I look ghastly! I visited the bathroom earlier and almost scared myself to death."

"Ruby! You're recovering from being poisoned. That'll take the wind out of anyone's sails. Pinch your cheeks to give you some colour." I settled on the end of her bed.

"It'll take more than that." She did as I suggested. "I've yet to see that dishy doctor from yesterday. I hope I didn't hallucinate him. He was divine. Tall, dark, handsome, and so gentle with his hands."

"Forget him. You're coming home with me to be thoroughly pampered."

"I'm looking forward to it," Ruby said. "Perhaps I should get ill more often if I'm treated like this."

"Let's not push our luck, shall we?" I smoothed her sheets. "Has the doctor been around yet?"

"He visited me half an hour ago. I got a clean bill of health. They're writing up the paperwork, and I have some pills to take home with me. Once they're collected, we can be on our way." She sighed. "I'll be glad of a comfortable bed and no nosy nurses coming to look at me."

"It's good they looked after you so carefully," I said. "What about Inspector Templeton? Has he been in yet?"

"No sign of him. Although I do want to talk to him. I was awake early, thinking about what I ate at the Craven Arms."

"What about your drinks?" I asked.

"I had two martinis, and they were delicious. I also snuck in a glass of wine. Joe uncorked an expensive bottle of wine and asked if I wanted a sneaky sip. I couldn't resist when he told me how much it cost."

I smacked a hand against my thigh. "I talked about this last night with Inspector Templeton. His men should have collected the empty wine bottle by now. They're testing it for strychnine. Grace Vilein gifted wine to Mr Lombard. She must have added the poison to the bottle."

"Gosh! I can well believe there was strychnine in it," Ruby said. "Joe only gave me half a glass. I had a few sips, but I didn't like the taste of it, so left the rest."

"I'm glad you did. If you'd finished it, you might not have survived." I stood and paced the room. "Ruby! We've solved the case. Grace was an obsessed fan, but something went wrong with their relationship and she decided to kill Mr Lombard."

"Grace was the older woman?" Ruby asked. "She seemed nervous and unsettled. Preferred her own company to spending time with us."

"Because she was hiding a guilty conscience." I paced some more. "Grace came to the ghost hunt with the sole purpose of poisoning Mr Lombard. She must have assumed he'd keep the bottle of wine to himself, drink it later that evening when he was alone."

"He was drinking wine before he began his vigil in the cellar," Ruby said.

"That's right! He must have decided he needed something to settle the nerves."

"What do you think went wrong between them?"

"We can figure that out once we get you home. You wait here. I'll collect your things and your pills, and we'll be on our way." I hurried out of the room. How quickly things changed. Last night, I was shaking with nerves, and now I shook with excitement. We'd uncovered the likely method of poisoning, and had a new prime suspect.

An hour later, Ruby was settled in one of the spare guest bedrooms in my family's home. She'd insisted on using the scant amount of makeup I owned to make herself look presentable and was drinking her third cup of sugary tea, which Matthew had brought her.

Matthew's adorable lame-footed puppy lolled on the end of her bed, enjoying all the attention he was getting from people coming and going.

"I would be perfectly content never to leave this place," Ruby said with a happy sigh. "So many treats. I feel like a princess."

"A poisoned princess," I murmured.

My mother bustled in, having almost leapt out of bed the second I'd brought Ruby home. She carried several books and a large blanket, which she covered Ruby with. "I don't want you getting cold. If you catch a chill in your weakened state, it'll be the end of you."

"Thank you, Edith," Ruby said. "And new mysteries to read. Wonderful. I'll enjoy getting stuck into those."

"Matthew's bringing through a gift." My mother continued to fuss with the blanket until she was satisfied Ruby was appropriately swaddled.

"Matthew bought me a gift?"

"He didn't buy it! The boy hasn't left the house in weeks. It's just been delivered. Here he is!"

Matthew struggled into the room with an enormous wicker hamper. "This is addressed to you." He set the large wicker hamper on the end of the bed and passed Ruby the card.

She took it with a delighted laugh and read it. "My goodness. How does Lady M know I'm here?"

"It's a food hamper," Matthew said. "I took a peek inside. It's all from Harrods."

"Perhaps Inspector Templeton told Lady M you were unwell," I said. "He could have instructed her to send any correspondence here."

My mother was peering through the contents of the hamper. "How generous of her. There's enough food in here to feed you for a month."

"We must share," Ruby said. "Is there chocolate? I'm craving something sweet."

"The doctor said plain food only," I said.

Ruby pouted. "One small chocolate. I almost died yesterday. A lady must have treats after such an ordeal."

"Of course she must." My mother was already unwrapping a large box of chocolates she'd pulled out of the hamper, which she handed to Ruby.

"Truffles. My absolute favourite," Ruby said.

I shook my head as my family suffocated Ruby with love. They adored her almost as much as I did, and I was glad I could bring her to a safe space to recover.

I stood and called Benji to my side.

Ruby looked up, her mouth full of chocolate. "You're not staying?"

"You're being well looked after," I said with affectionate exasperation. "And I have plans today. I'm catching a killer and making them sorry they ever hurt my best friend."

Chapter 12

I sat at my desk in the London Times office, tapping my fingers on the hard wooden surface as I was kept on hold for the third time while waiting to speak to Inspector Templeton. What was taking him so long? Mr Lombard's murder and Ruby's poisoning must be his top priority, but the man didn't have the common decency to keep me informed as to what was going on.

Had our conversation last night meant nothing? Maybe his men had failed to find the wine bottle that contained the poison, and he was too fearful to tell me. We should have gone back to the Craven Arms as soon as we'd uncovered that possibility. This was a failing on my part, letting my tiredness get the better of me.

At last, the telephone connected.

I didn't wait for an introduction. "It's Veronica. What news do you have?"

"I know exactly who this is. If you keep telephoning me so regularly, people will talk. They're already gossiping at the reception, asking if we're familiar with each other."

I tutted. "I care nothing for idle gossip. And your officers should be working, not idling about stirring the rumour pot. Did you find the wine bottle?"

"Of course. That's why I've been busy. As I told you I would, I sent two of my best men to the Craven Arms. Joe wasn't happy about being disturbed, but he understood the importance of assisting us."

"I had no doubt he'd oblige you. Joe is an excellent chap. What do the tests show?"

Inspector Templeton huffed out his irritation. "I'm unable to click my fingers and produce tests in a matter of hours. It may have escaped your attention, but this isn't the only investigation I'm working on."

"It's your most important investigation," I said. "A murder and the poisoning of a most excellent woman must take precedence over everything else. Ruby told me she drank some of the wine, so the connection is clear."

"That information is useful, but it proves nothing." Inspector Templeton sighed heavily, and I could picture him pinching the bridge of his nose with his eyes shut in exasperation at my persistence. "I have three drownings, two deaths by violent means, an investigation involving a possible opioid overdose, two suspicious child deaths, and an unfortunate incident involving an out-of-control motorcar. They all require my attention."

"I'm sorry those dreadful things have happened. Get your men to work. You're not supposed to do everything single-handed, are you?"

"I don't. But there are only so many of us to go around. I've urged the team to conduct the tests on the wine bottle as swiftly as possible."

It wasn't an acceptable option, but it appeared it was the only one I'd be offered. "And when will the results be back?"

"The best answer I can give you is soon. I submitted the request first thing this morning."

"Are you checking to make sure they're not idling and gossiping about us?"

"Veronica! If it wasn't rude, I'd hang up on you. Let my people do their jobs. And please, let me do mine. Your constant telephone calls are distracting. I need quiet so I can focus."

I was not deterred by his stern tone. "What about Grace? Have you brought her in for questioning?"

"Until we have the results back on the bottle of wine, there's no point in questioning her. I already have her original statement."

"That's it? Shouldn't you bring her in? She could become worried you're onto her and make a run for it."

"Grace doesn't strike me as a running kind of woman. And she has responsibilities at home," Inspector Templeton said.

"A family to care for?"

"Her elderly parents. Nothing we've said to her will make her concerned that we consider her a suspect. And, just to be clear, although we've discussed Grace's involvement in this crime, until there is absolute evidence she put poison in the wine bottle, she is guilty of nothing."

"I know about being innocent until proven guilty." I scowled to myself, causing Benji to whine and rest his chin on my knee, sensing my distress. His thoughtful sweetness cooled my irritation. "I don't mean to be curt, but I was so worried about Ruby. It's never hit home like this before."

"Murder is a serious business. And the people who conduct it are usually dangerous or unstable. Give me time to collect more evidence, and attempt nothing unwise while I'm doing so."

"Inspector! I never do anything unwise. My methods and actions are always well thought out."

"Was that the case when you were hit on the head with a tree branch whilst chasing someone?"

I delicately sniffed. "That was a lapse of judgement. It happens a few times a year at most. And sometimes, when one is startled, one makes foolish decisions."

"Don't make any foolish decisions with this investigation," Inspector Templeton said. "And you must have work to occupy your time until I have news for you."

"The dead are in no hurry." My gaze flicked to Bob, who lurked nearby, a notepad in one hand. He gestured for me to finish my telephone call. The cheek of the man.

"When I hear anything, I'll let you know," Inspector Templeton said. "In the meantime, keep your head down and cause no trouble. How is Ruby?"

"Doing marvellously. Thank you for asking. I extracted her from the hospital first thing this morning, and she is being spoiled by my mother and Matthew. I assume you told Lady M about Ruby's whereabouts. She received a huge Harrods gift hamper."

"Lady M is well connected, and when she heard rumours of Ruby's misfortune, she contacted my superior. In turn, I got a flea in my ear while still in my pyjamas and before my morning coffee. She's as stern as you when making demands, and she insisted on updates until we uncover the murderer."

"I'm glad Ruby has so many champions," I said. "It'll ensure a job well done."

"With you and the indomitable Lady M hassling me, I won't sleep until this case is solved."

"That's the spirit." Bob was creeping closer. "I must go. My apologies for being an irritation. I'm aware how taxing they can be."

Inspector Templeton inhaled. "You're never an irritation. But your strong will would test a saint."

"It's a good job you aren't a saint." We said our goodbyes, and I hung up the telephone. "Is there something you need, Bob?"

"Your interview for my article."

"Must it be now?"

"Unless you want me to miss the deadline. You can explain to Harry how you made things difficult for me, so I was unable to do my job. It'll be another black mark on your record."

"My record is pristine, as well you know."

He scrubbed a chubby finger under his nose. "Comes with having an uncle who owns the paper, I suppose."

"If you intend to insult me, you'll get nothing other than no comment."

Bob's top lip curled. "Let's make this quick, so it's less painful for both of us."

I checked the time. I had an appointment in just over an hour, but I could squeeze Bob in. And he wouldn't leave me alone until I'd answered his questions. "Very well. Ask away."

He flipped open his notepad and licked the end of his pencil. "How scared were you on the ghost hunt?"

"Not scared at all."

"You must believe in ghosts, though, since you were there."

"I keep an open mind on as many things as possible. Having never seen evidence of ghosts, it's hard to believe they exist."

He scribbled away in his messy shorthand. "Since your family owns the Craven Arms, you must have been there plenty of times. You've never seen anything troubling?"

"If by troubling, you mean a floating apparition or a wailing woman, then no. The worst we've had to deal with were mice in the cellar."

"I'll write down that you've seen several strange things and were so scared during the hunt, you almost fainted."

I pulled back my shoulders. "You will do no such thing."

"We need to make the story interesting, or we won't sell copies," Bob said. "Nothing about the evening unsettled you? Come on, use your imagination."

"A man dead at the bottom of the cellar steps was unsettling," I said.

"What about his ghost? Did you see it emerge from the body?"

I sighed. "Now you're being ridiculous. If you have no sensible questions, go back to your desk and stop bothering me."

Bob glowered at me as he scribbled some more, no doubt making up lies to put in his article. "Harry's been talking to the old bill about the dead guy."

"I assumed he would." Uncle Harry had connections everywhere to ensure all the stories we published were credible.

"They're talking about the death being deliberate, not an accident. Is there anything you want to add to that? Did you see what happened? Were you involved?" Bob leered at me.

"The police know far more than me. And as for me being a suspect, I've been ruled out."

"You're as thick as thieves with one of the local inspectors. What secrets has he told you about the death?"

I couldn't stop my smile. "If I told you, it wouldn't be a secret."

"You're the worst interviewee I've ever dealt with." Bob flipped his notepad shut.

"I could say the same about the interviewer. You'll write whatever you like, no matter what I say."

"Readers need titillation."

"You should work at Isabella's newspaper if that's the kind of nonsense you wish to write," I said.

Bob glared at me as he pulled up the waistband of his sagging trousers. "I have to write you were a little scared, or you'll seem unnatural."

"Because I should be a delicate woman who is unable to cope with being in the dark while hearing lurid tales of things that don't exist?"

Bob pointed his pencil at me. "Exactly! I'll write that, but cut out the last part. You believe in ghosts and feared for your life."

I turned towards him. "What about you? Do you believe in ghosts?"

He shrugged. "I believe in whatever sells newspapers."

It was a wicked thing to do, but Bob deserved teasing. "I heard there's a ghost local to this area who enjoys bothering jaded middle-aged men who are rude to women."

He tucked his pencil behind his ear and smirked at me. "I can imagine you coming back as that sort of ghost. Shrewish and sharp. Mean to all men and scaring them away with your waspish attitude."

"I'll only haunt the people who irritated me the most when I was alive." I looked over his shoulder and faked shock. "You should watch out. The ghost could be here right now. Have you noticed a drop in temperature? And what is that strange smell?"

"You're out of your mind, you are." Bob glanced over his shoulder. "If I need anything else, I'll come back."

"I'll be out. I have work to do." I'd arranged to meet Mr Lombard's publisher, Nicholas, at his office on Green Lane. When I'd contacted him, I'd said I needed background details for the obituary. He'd only afforded me a fifteen-minute appointment, but that was all I needed.

I left Benji with Uncle Harry, caught a cab outside the London Times, and hopped out at the publishing house. It was a small, pleasant brown brick building with well-tended flowers outside. I was greeted by an efficient receptionist, who took my details and told me to take a seat.

A moment later, Nicholas came out of his office wearing a pinstripe suit, his silver hair slicked back in the fashion of the time.

"Hold my calls. I want to give Miss Vale my full attention." Nicholas greeted me with a handshake and led me into his office. It was an expensively decorated room, with dark teak furnishings and a large leather chair set behind a desk.

"Thank you for seeing me so swiftly," I said.

"Anything for William." Nicholas gestured to a seat, then took his own behind the desk. "Although, I'd appreciate it if you were straight to the point. I have a busy afternoon. Wall-to-wall appointments."

I respected a forthright approach. I took out my notepad and placed it on my knee. "When we spoke at the Craven Arms, you mentioned the inconvenience caused by Mr Lombard's death."

Nicholas startled, before smoothing a hand over his hair. "I spoke out of turn. It was the shock. I didn't mean to appear heartless. Although we had a professional relationship, I considered him a good sort. We'd often dine together, share a laugh, and enjoy a cigar."

"If you don't mind me saying, you didn't appear distressed when Mr Lombard's body was discovered in the cellar."

"Again, shock. And people behave differently when faced with a traumatic situation."

"What was your opinion of Mr Lombard's area of expertise?" I asked.

He quirked an eyebrow. "You're asking me if I believe in ghosts?"

I nodded.

"To be truthful, the paranormal is a trendy subject. People clamour to read stories about ghosts."

"You're only in it for the money?"

"It's one of my motivations. People cannot live without money. Ghosts are a passing trend, just like every other fictional topic. I'm unsure why they're of such interest at the moment, though. Perhaps lonely types seeking comfort after the Great War. So many people were lost, and there are questions that need answering. Lots of men were never found and are still listed as missing when we know what really happened to them."

"Sadly, we do. It strikes me as tragic that you make money from such a situation."

"I make no apologies for being a capitalist. The more money I make, the more I can give back."

"You're charitable?"

"When I have a mind to be." Nicholas offered me a cigarette from a silver case, but I declined. "What does any of this have to do with William's obituary?"

"I'm getting a fuller picture of your relationship," I said. "I like to ensure anyone who had a special connection with the dearly departed is mentioned in the obituary."

"Of course." Nicholas checked the time. "Was there anything else?"

"Was Mr Lombard always punctual when providing material? I recall you saying something about him being behind on his latest book."

A hint of anger flashed across Nicholas's face. "That's the trouble with artistic types. Deadlines don't inspire them. They need a nudge of encouragement to get the words down on paper."

"How did you nudge Mr Lombard?"

"I took him to dinner at the Savoy." Nicholas smiled. "Naturally, it was a business expense, but it was an enjoyable way to convince him to give me the final chapters of his new book."

"How late was he in delivering them?"

Nicholas sighed. "Three months. And he'd already been paid an advance. It was the main reason I organised the readings and book tour around London. I needed to make sure his fans didn't forget him, so the new book wouldn't flop when it finally came out."

I made a note of his comments, but also jotted down that this was a possible motive. If Mr Lombard had become an expensive liability, it might have been cheaper to get rid of him and use his death as a publicity stunt to boost sales.

"I don't recall seeing you when Mr Lombard was first found in the cellar," I said.

"When William took a tumble, I was outside having a smoke."

Was that a handy convenience? Perhaps he'd assumed if he wasn't seen at the crime scene, he couldn't be involved in the murder.

"If you have no more questions, I need to get on," Nicholas said. "I've got a new client visiting."

"Thank you. I have everything I need." I shook his hand and left the office. I nodded to the receptionist and headed into the corridor, almost bumping into George Cloister.

"Hello! You're the gal from the other night at the haunted pub."

"That's right. Veronica Vale. I was getting a few words from Nicholas for Mr Lombard's obituary."

"Ah! Of course. Terrible business. If you'll excuse me." Mr Cloister sidled past and disappeared into the office.

I walked along the corridor, glancing over my shoulder now and again. Mr Lombard was being replaced by Mr Cloister? Even though Grace was my prime suspect, I couldn't discount the possibility that the exasperated publisher and the rival ghost hunter were in on it together.

Chapter 13

After returning to work, I'd barely been able to focus on my obituaries, even though there was a fascinating death concerning a young lady in a pink gown, found in a shallow pond at a nearby mansion.

I kept returning to my concerns about Grace. I'd telephoned Inspector Templeton three times during the afternoon to find out what was going on, but he'd refused to speak to me.

As tempting as it was to march to the police station and demand answers, it would only irritate him. So, I took matters into my own hands. I made a discreet call to the directory and obtained Grace's home address. I was fortunate she had such an unusual surname, and there were only three Vileins in the whole of London, all living at the same address. An address not far from the Craven Arms.

I presented my obituaries to Uncle Harry, bid him farewell, and dashed out of the office with Benji. The evening was cool and clear, so we made the forty-five-minute journey to Grace's house on foot to get some much-needed exercise. Sitting at a desk all day was dreadful for my posture, and Benji had been fretting for a long walk all afternoon.

I double-checked the address before knocking at number fourteen Osman Road. It was one of numerous terraces on a tidy street in a respectable part of London. The windows were clean, and the entranceway recently swept, suggesting Grace took pride in her home.

The door was opened not by Grace, but by a grey-haired lady wearing a flowered housecoat and beige slippers. "May I help you?"

"I hope so. I'm looking for Grace." I introduced myself and Benji. "Is she home?"

"She is." The woman was past sixty, with a wrinkled face and hands and thin lips. "Are you a friend from her place of work? I've not seen you here before."

"No, we don't work together. We met recently at an event, and I wanted to see how Grace was feeling," I said.

The woman regarded me sternly, and was silent for so long, I wondered if she was going to answer. "She's in bed because of her headache."

"I'm sorry to hear that." Another silence stretched between us. "Are you her mother?"

She nodded. "Mrs Vilein."

I looked past her, waiting for an invitation. None came.

"Perhaps I could visit Grace? The company may cheer her up."

Mrs Vilein sighed. "Come in. Make sure your dog behaves, or he'll have to go outside."

"Benji is always on his best behaviour."

She eyed him with suspicion before moving to one side. "Grace hasn't gotten out of bed all day. She even insisted I go to the end of the road and use the telephone box to let her employer know she wouldn't be in. Grace rarely misses a day of work, so she must be feeling poorly."

I stepped into a narrow hallway with clean tiles underfoot and faded flower-patterned wallpaper. There was a hint of aged Victorian decor, but everything was tidy and in its place. I hung my coat and handbag on the peg as directed and followed Mrs Vilein along the hallway as she shuffled her slippered feet, suggesting walking was uncomfortable.

"Don't make too much noise. My husband's fallen asleep after eating his tea. I was supposed to listen to the radio this evening, but I won't hear a thing over his snoring."

"I'll be sure not to bother him," I said. "Is it just the three of you who live here?"

"That's right. We moved in after we got married. Grace has never married, so she stays with us. And I'm glad of it. Now we're older, we need looking after. It's only right, isn't it? I cared for Grace when she was young, so she does the same for us. It's a child's obligation."

I didn't agree. If the only reason people had children was to have a free nurse on hand in their old age, it seemed frightfully unfair. But rather than saying as much, I simply nodded.

"This is her." Mrs Vilein knocked on a closed door. "Grace, you've got company."

"I'm not well."

"You'll feel better for seeing your friend." She pushed open the door to reveal a bedroom with pink walls and a vast array of doilies covering nearly every surface.

It was a cornucopia of wool and yarn in every colour imaginable.

Grace was tucked under the covers, her expression turning to surprise when she saw me. "Goodness! What are you doing here?"

"That's no way to greet a friend," Mrs Vilein said. "Miss Vale wanted to see how you were feeling."

"Don't believe what she told you!" Grace gripped her sheets.

"Whatever are you talking about? Miss Vale said you met at an event. Although I'm unsure what event. The only thing you've been to recently is your knitting circle. Do you knit, Miss Vale?"

"Whenever I try, I drop stitches."

"You didn't meet at the knitting circle?" Mrs Vilein's expression hardened. "Grace, you've not been telling untruths, have you? Not chasing around after that ne'er-do-well who spouts lies about ghosts? I've warned you about him."

Grace's cheeks flushed. "I'm a grown woman. I can choose my own interests."

Mrs Vilein sighed and crossed her arms over her chest. "It's unnatural to believe such nonsense. Leave the dead where they belong. Why bother them?"

"You don't hold the same beliefs as Grace?" I asked.

"Of course not. All this ghost bothering business is unnatural. My parents worked the land, so I've seen the cycle of life and death hundreds of times. There's no such thing as ghosts."

"Don't say that!" Grace said. "We don't know what happens after we die. We could learn valuable information from ghosts."

Mrs Vilein snorted. "The dead don't talk. There's nothing to learn. What's dead, stays dead."

"I've heard them," Grace muttered.

Mrs Vilein glanced at me. "We're simple folk with simple beliefs. My dad was a farm labourer, and there were six of us to raise, so my ma had her hands full."

"I imagine she did," I said.

Her expression softened a fraction. "Grace and my old ma were close. I was poorly after Grace was born, and my ma came to stay and help out. She ended up staying for ten years. I didn't mind, although it got crowded."

"I loved my grandma," Grace said. "I was heartbroken when she died."

"We all were," Mrs Vilein said. "But she's gone. She's been gone a long time. Grace has never accepted that. She still talks to her."

Grace nodded. "Grandma was kind, and she encouraged me. She told me I could make something of my life. I feel like I've let her down."

"Stop talking rubbish," Mrs Vilein said. "You have a good life, and you're a good girl. You help take care of us. There's nothing kinder than that."

Grace huffed, seeming more like a young person than a mature woman ten years my senior. "There's more to life than this."

"You can have your freedom when we're dead and in the ground. Until then, you have obligations. No more arguing. It never gets us anywhere other than snapping at each other. Miss Vale, if you're staying, I'll brew a pot of tea." Mrs Vilein bustled off, putting an end to her dispute with Grace.

I eased the door closed so we could converse in private. "I'm sorry if my visit causes trouble for you. That wasn't my intention."

Grace looked away. "I'm really not feeling well."

"I won't stay long. I wanted to know more about Mr Lombard. When we spoke at the Craven Arms, you said you followed his ghost hunts around London."

She still didn't meet my gaze. "What if I did? Everyone is allowed hobbies. Although the way my parents talk, you wouldn't believe it. They think my only hobby is to take care of them."

"It's good you do that, but it's also nice to have other interests. One that allows you to follow a passion."

"My parents think it's ridiculous. They've forbidden me from going to ghost hunts." Grace cast me a guilty look. "It's why I tell them I'm in a knitting circle. It's about the only thing they think is good for me."

I glanced around Grace's bedroom. It was outfitted for a young girl, with affectations of youthful activities. There were children's picture books on the shelf, and images of bunnies and kittens on the walls.

"I'm sure your parents behave that way because they want to protect you," I said. "Many are unsettled by the thought of ghosts."

"They're unsettled by anything modern. And I'm stuck with them because I'm an unmarried spinster. I should be allowed time off to do something enjoyable. Ghosts fascinate me."

"Just like Mr Lombard. I'm writing his obituary, and I'm looking for comments from people who knew him."

"Oh! I'll be in his obituary?" Grace's expression brightened.

"You may not be named, but I always gather a full picture of the deceased so I can do them justice." I took out my notepad. "I understand you gave Mr Lombard gifts when you attended the ghost hunts."

"Yes! I knew all his favourite things." A teary smile crossed Grace's face. "And I followed him everywhere. Well, everywhere I could get to and back within a day. I rarely leave my parents overnight. They don't like it."

"How many times have you attended an investigation?"

"Seven times this year! William had a wonderful way with ghosts, and he was an incredible writer. I have all of his books." Grace pointed to the bookcase. "They're signed. I had to queue for hours once to get a signature, but it was worth it."

"Did you give him a gift when you visited the Craven Arms?" I asked.

"Yes, a bottle of wine. I read about his favourite tipple in a book. He said he often treated himself to a glass of wine before tackling difficult spirits."

"Was it an expensive bottle?"

Her cheeks coloured. "I don't mind spending money on William. He was so good to me, and we shared a fascination with ghosts. And I save most of my money from my job because I don't pay rent. Well, I pay because I look after my parents, but everything I have goes into savings. There's no harm in treating someone you admire, is there?"

"Absolutely not. I'm sure Mr Lombard was thrilled to receive such a generous gift." It was curious how willing Grace was to reveal she'd gifted the wine. If she'd added the poison, surely, she'd have concealed the information. After all, she wasn't to know I was well acquainted with the police, so I had insider knowledge.

Grace reached for a handkerchief and dabbed her nose. "It's silly, getting upset over a man I didn't really know, but he's been a big part of my life. My gran died a long time ago, but I miss her something terrible."

Benji settled his head on the edge of her bed and gently licked her hand.

Grace smiled and patted him.

"Losing a loved one is always hard," I said. "You never really forget them."

She looked up at me. "Have you lost someone?"

"My father."

"I'm sorry to hear that."

"It was some time ago, but he's always close by, guiding me."

"You've seen his ghost?" Grace's eyes went wide.

"Oh, no, not like that. But he was a kind and generous man. He always encouraged me to learn, grow, and discover my talents and interests."

Grace fiddled with a thread on her sheet. "My mother underplayed my grandma's role in my life. She was really sick after she had me and didn't get out of bed for almost a year. My grandma was always there for me, making sure I got fed and had clean clothes. She never complained once. She was so warm and loving."

"Your grandmother sounds like a wonderful person."

"She was. And she always wanted the best for me. She'd buy me books about explorers and their adventures around the world. Places I would never visit. Australia, Africa, even the Antarctic. We'd sit together and plan my trips. Then she died, and that went away.

My parents got rid of those books and said they were ridiculous fantasies."

"A double loss to have your dreams taken from you."

"My heart broke, and it never recovered." Grace wiped her eyes. "When I got older, I learned there were people who talked to ghosts. That's when I visited William for the first time."

"You had private sittings with him?" I asked.

"At least once a month. I enjoyed the ghost hunts, but William could tap into the spirit world and reach out to those who'd passed over. He was my connection to my grandma."

It now made sense why Mr Lombard had recognised Grace when she asked her question after the book reading. "Extraordinary. Did you ever get to communicate with your grandma?"

"Yes! And she knew things about me that William couldn't possibly have known. She'd talk to me about making travel plans. She saw I was sad and felt trapped. I was thrilled to hear from her." Grace's cheeks flushed with colour again. "I should be grateful for what I have, and my parents aren't unkind, but they don't understand me. Not the way my grandma did."

"It must have been comforting to communicate with her," I said as sincerely as possible. And remarkably clever of Mr Lombard to convince Grace he was speaking to her dead grandmother.

"William meant everything to me because he was a link to the woman who raised me." She sniffled into her handkerchief. "Now, he's gone, and I don't know what I'll do. Have I lost her for good this time?"

"Perhaps you could find another ghost communicator?"

Grace shook her head. "I visited a few before I found William, but they weren't honest. He was the first spirit communicator I believed in."

Mrs Vilein interrupted the conversation by bringing in a tea tray. She passed around cups of stewed steaming brew the colour of dark stained oak. "You've got a hint of life in those pale cheeks," she said to Grace. "Having a friend visit is doing you good. Even if that friend believes in all the ghost rubbish."

Grace lowered her gaze as she sipped her tea, not seeming to have the energy to engage in more verbal sparring.

While we exchanged pleasantries and conveniently sidestepped the topic of the paranormal, settling on the weather and how well-mannered Benji was, my mind whirled. Grace had been open about giving gifts to Mr Lombard. She hadn't flinched or seemed concerned when I mentioned the bottle of wine. And Mr Lombard had done her a great service by giving her hope that she was still in touch with a dearly loved relative.

Had something gone wrong to sour the relationship? Mr Lombard's lies had been uncovered, so Grace sought her revenge. Or was I looking at this investigation all wrong?

Chapter 14

"If you feed that puppy another piece of sausage, it'll go pop." I smiled indulgently as Ruby tickled our foster pup and snuck him yet another treat.

"No one can resist this adorable face," she said. "And he's barely left my side since I've been recovering."

"Neither has my mother, but I don't see you feeding her sausage."

"Veronica! Behave yourself." My mother was back in her usual place, tucked under her covers, while we all lounged on the end of her bed, enjoying an early breakfast with Matthew, the foster pup, and Benji.

Ruby shot me a mildly exasperated look from beneath her eyelashes. "Your mother's care is welcome."

"I had to make sure you didn't expire in my best guest bedroom," my mother said. "I can't have that on my conscience, especially since Matthew has been no good at ensuring you keep breathing."

"I've made all the meals!" he said. "And I even called out of the front door and got that boy to get us fresh bread when Ruby ate the last slice."

"It would have done you no harm to take the short walk along the street and collect it yourself," I said. "The baker is friendly."

Matthew ruffled the puppy's fur. "I've been too busy looking after this little guy. His leg isn't getting any better."

I sighed as I inspected the adorable little creature. "I don't want to put him through surgery, but it may come to it."

"Will they remove the leg?" my mother asked.

"The vets at the dogs' home do wonderful things. But if it does have to come off, I know many dogs who thrive with three limbs. They still run and play."

"He's too much of a baby to go through that trauma." Ruby cuddled the puppy and got her chin licked.

As my family lavished the delighted puppy with attention, I gently stroked Benji, who was content to lean against my leg and eat the occasional sausage treat. He was a confident dog, never growing jealous, even when there was an adorable puppy or kitten in residence who took everyone's attention.

"I'll be able to help with the investigation now I'm back on my feet," Ruby said.

"You are looking better," I said. "No more aches and pains?"

"I had a few tingles in my fingers, but that's gone now. The doctor said I may have a few aftershocks, but it was nothing to worry about unless it got worse or I felt too stiff to move."

"You should rest for at least a month to ensure your constitution is fully restored," my mother said. "You don't want a relapse. I've done that to myself so many times. Gotten out of bed when it was the last thing I should have done. I've set myself back months with headaches, tremors, and terrible palpitations."

"I hope I haven't put you under too much strain by being here," Ruby said. "You've been so good to me. My parents will be eternally grateful. Although I've yet to tell them I was poisoned. I'm tempted not to, since they've got enough on their plates."

"Problems at home?" I asked.

Ruby played with the puppy's floppy ears. "Their trip to Scotland didn't reveal the rewards they'd hoped for, so it's back to the drawing board."

"Is your father still inventing things?" my mother asked.

"He never stops! And that's part of the trouble. Father never finishes a thing. He bounces from one idea to the other like an excitable puppy, and when he submits the patents, they're rejected because they're incomplete. The man is a genius, but he needs someone with a business head to ensure he settles to a project's completion."

"He should write a book, like Mr Lombard did," Matthew said. "Tell people how to invent things."

"He hasn't the dedication. Father never sits still for more than five minutes. He's always swinging his arms around and yelling about something exciting he's discovered and how we must see it. I adore him, but his lack of focus is irritating."

I suppressed a smile. Ruby was known for getting distracted, too. Especially when there was a new handbag to be inspected. "My meeting with Mr Lombard's publisher proved fruitful. Nicholas was having trouble getting the final chapters of the latest ghost book. Apparently, he had to bribe Mr Lombard with meals at the Savoy to get him to cooperate."

"What a treat," Ruby said. "We should dine there. Although, I'll need to save up. The food is delicious, but jolly expensive."

"We'll put it in the diary. On my way out of that meeting, I bumped into George Cloister. He clearly had an appointment with Nicholas. And it got me wondering. Did they conspire to get rid of Mr Lombard because he was a liability?"

"Find a new star and snuff out the old one?" Ruby asked. "How callous. Do you still have doubts about Grace's guilt?"

"Increasingly so since speaking to her," I said.

"Any more news about the poison?" Matthew asked.

"We've discovered how it was administered," I said. "And thank you for reminding me. I must telephone Inspector Templeton for an update. He's been remiss in keeping us informed of his progress."

"He's a terrible stinker for not telling you his every move," Ruby said with a grin.

"It's most frustrating." I slid off the bed while they talked about poisons and how long Ruby should remain on her sickbed, and walked into the hall where the telephone was located.

I contacted Inspector Templeton so regularly that I knew his number by heart. I was put through to his line by a tired-sounding policeman. When it finally connected, a loud sigh came down the telephone line.

"Good morning to you, too, Inspector," I said. "I'm sure you're not surprised to hear from me."

"If it's about the wine bottle, there are still no results back," he said.

"What are your chaps doing? They'd better not be sleeping on the job."

"I assure you, they're not. But our lord and master is pressing hard for the slum clearance to happen as soon as possible. Many of us are working double shifts to keep on top of things."

"You don't need your laboratory types doing that. They aren't skilled in manual labour."

"True, but when an old tenement building was cleared, officers found sick people hiding there, and there are concerns they could be infectious. They've been hospitalised, and tests are being run. The officers who found them have been taken off duty in case they're contagious, too. It's left us in a hole."

"How dreadful. I hope they make a full recovery."

"They should be fine. It's just a precaution. Is Ruby still on the mend?"

"She's having the time of her life staying here," I said fondly. "You'd never know she'd been poisoned. She wants to get back to work, but my mother isn't keen on letting her leave. I imagine she's enjoying the company."

"Tell Ruby to take it slow. Although if she's anything like you, she won't listen to my advice," Inspector Templeton said.

"I always listen to sensible advice, as does Ruby," I said. "And in the spirit of this companionable bond, I should inform you, I visited Grace yesterday."

"I'm too tired to be annoyed by this news," he said. "Did you learn anything useful?"

"Grace is sad and angry in equal measure. She was in bed with a headache and feeling pathetic. She adored Mr Lombard and is frustrated by her situation, stuck at home, caring for her elderly parents. Having met her mother, it seems she guilted her into staying to care for them as they age."

"I can think of worse things for an unmarried daughter with few complications," Inspector Templeton said.

"There's always room for kindness, but it should cut both ways. Grace has barely lived. She's never married, and her bedroom is full of childish things. She hasn't been given an opportunity to experience life."

"Sometimes, real life isn't all it's cracked up to be. Why shouldn't her parents want to shield her from the worst of it?"

I twisted the telephone cable around a finger. "It seems like a life wasted."

"Grace won't miss seeing the poverty and problems rife beneath the glossy veneer that's been painted after the war." Inspector Templeton's tone was unusually morose. "Everyone thinks life is easy now the Great War is over, but there's so much devastation left behind, and we're picking up the pieces."

"Yes, that is tough. And it sounds as if you got out of bed on the wrong side this morning."

"I haven't been to bed. There's a detective off sick, several others pulled into the slum clearance, and new cases arrived overnight."

"You poor chap. They must let you rest. You won't be able to do your job if you're not getting enough sleep. And you can't afford to make an error with this investigation. I won't allow my best friend to be poisoned without bringing down hellfire and brimstone on the villain."

"I'll tell the chief that. Perhaps he'll want to employ you."

"Hah! He couldn't keep up with me. Although I'd be happy to speak to him and tell him what for. Make sure he takes better care of his employees."

Inspector Templeton chuckled. "I don't doubt you would. While I've been waiting for the results on the wine bottle, I looked into Grace's background. There's no criminal history, but she is in considerable debt."

"What is the debt set against?"

"As yet unknown. But she withdrew several large sums from her bank. Where the money went after that is a mystery."

"Grace told me she saved her money," I said. "But I can tell you one thing. Those withdrawals weren't an investment in the house she lives in. When I visited, everything was neat and tidy, but faded. They're a family who make do and mend rather than buy new. And as I mentioned, Grace's room hasn't been altered for at least thirty years. Perhaps she bought a vehicle."

"There's nothing registered in her name or in her parents' names," Inspector Templeton said.

"Health problems? They needed access to urgent treatment, so secured the services of a private doctor."

"Did either of the parents seem unwell?"

"The mother was hearty enough. I didn't meet Grace's father. He was asleep. But there was no mention of ill health. Although Grace had a headache, I didn't detect any serious illness among the family."

"I've got a chap looking into medical records to see if that's the cause of the expense," Inspector Templeton said. "We can also rule out a property purchase. It wouldn't have been enough for a deposit."

"Grace isn't looking to rent her own home. Her parents won't let her fly the nest. Her mother stated she could live once they were dead, and not before."

"I've arranged to visit Grace and see what else I can learn," Inspector Templeton said.

"Although I only saw her yesterday, I'd be happy to come with you."

"There's no need."

"You said yourself, you're shorthanded, and Grace is a meek sort of woman. You'll need a feminine touch to cajole answers from her."

"I have female police officers if I need that. You stick to what you're best at."

"Solving your crimes?"

He sighed again. "Goodbye, Veronica."

The line went dead, but I smiled as I set the telephone back in the cradle. I felt a touch sorry for Inspector Templeton. He was being pulled in different directions, and he had me bothering him. But I'll continue to do so until this puzzle was resolved to my satisfaction.

I returned to the bedroom to find Matthew had cleared the breakfast things. My mother was half asleep, and Ruby was fussing the puppy.

"Any news from your inspector?" Ruby asked.

"No updates on the poison. Inspector Templeton is still focused on Grace."

"You hear people talk about poison being a woman's method of murder," Ruby said. "Something about it being a sly way to kill. I've always thought that was impolite."

"We can be a tad sneaky, but women can be as violent as men," I said. "We discovered that when we uncovered Florence Sterling's murderer not so long ago."

"When our anger is roused, we're glorious Furies," Ruby said. "And I, for one, can hold a grudge like nobody else. I'm the opposite of my brother. Todd forgives everyone, no matter how rotten they are to him. He's a soft-hearted ninny."

"You forgive too," I said.

"Not the cads who break my heart." Ruby checked the time. "I should telephone Lady M. I think I'll try a morning of work and see how I get on. Nothing vigorous, but there is always paperwork that needs my attention."

My mother woke herself with a loud snore and lurched in the bed. "What did I miss?"

"Nothing of note," I said. "You rest some more. Eating so much breakfast is taxing."

"Cheeky girl," she said. "And Ruby, it's back to bed for you."

"I'm ready to face the world again," she said. "What about you, Veronica?"

"After work, if you're up for a challenge, we're visiting a ghost's great-granddaughter."

Chapter 15

Work had been busy but a touch dull. I hadn't had a single exciting obituary. The deaths had all been remarkably conventional, involving failed hearts or old age. I always imagined my death being quick and painless. I wouldn't want to drag myself through old age with illnesses, ailments, and complaints. And I certainly didn't intend to do anything as mean-spirited as Grace's parents and guilt a family member into looking after me if my health failed.

We all deserved freedom and happiness, so I intended to live a full life and go out with a bang. What that bang would consist of, I hadn't figured out.

For once, Ruby was on time, and was parked outside the front of the London Times office as I exited the building with Benji.

She gave me a cheery wave and gestured me over, calling out through the open window. "The traffic is terrible, so I brought food for the journey."

"My goodness. What got you here so promptly?" I slid into the luxurious passenger seat of her Ghost, after settling Benji in the back on the tartan rug Ruby kept in the vehicle for just such a special guest.

"Being poisoned has given me a new outlook on life." Ruby eased the car into the busy traffic, but not before placing a brown paper bag of chocolate lime sweets onto my lap.

"Staring death in the face has made you a better timekeeper?" I asked.

Ruby chuckled. "Alas, it wasn't the poison. Lady M was an absolute treat all day. She wouldn't let me do anything strenuous and even came to the stables and barked orders at the terrified stable boys. She tried to get one poor lad involved in the filing. After ten minutes of watching him disastrously fumble with the paperwork, I took pity on him."

"I knew Lady M had a heart," I said.

"She's a steely old thing, but a treasure when the chips are down. She insisted I put my feet up and only work for ten minutes every hour. I even had an afternoon nap. And she ordered in a delicious cream tea with five different types of jam. After we'd eaten, she said I could leave early."

"I'm glad she took care of you," I said.

"I should say she did. And Lady M shocked me by saying I was the daughter she'd never had. I always thought she didn't like me since she's always snapping at me."

"Maybe that's her way of showing she cares." I unwrapped a sweet and passed it to Ruby before taking my own. Lady M was an old-school Victorian widow who'd inherited vast sums of money from her late husband. She'd invested that money into her one passion: horses. And when Ruby and Lady M had met at a garden party, an acquaintance was struck over their interest in equines.

Ruby yawned as she drove along a quieter stretch of road.

"Even though you've been taking it easy, I can drop you back at mine. I don't want you overexerting yourself," I said.

"I'll be fine. I'm looking forward to doing something active. I've eaten too much today, and my figure's not as forgiving as it used to be." She tugged at the waistband of her soft grey A-line midi skirt.

"We won't be long. I've been researching Millicent and her family in between writing obituaries. They have a fascinating history."

"Is that where Millicent gets her feistiness from?" Ruby asked. "She wasn't afraid to put Nicholas in his place when we were at the Craven Arms."

"Perhaps so. According to my research, her great-grandmother, who allegedly haunts my pub, was a highway robber. One of only a few female highway robbers ever recorded in the history books."

"How extraordinary! I didn't know women were involved in such a thing."

"Annie Crophampton, her married name, was notorious for robbing the rich. She was a criminal with a conscience. She only took from those who could afford it, and donated generously to local causes, including the parish church close to the Craven Arms. Apparently, when they rebuilt a section of the church following storm damage, the mayor had a foundation stone inserted with Annie's name inscribed on it because she was such a generous benefactor."

"A thief with a heart," Ruby said. "They're the best kind."

"Sadly, Annie's luck ran out when she was captured. And there used to be gallows close to the Craven Arms. She was hanged there."

"Was Annie a regular at the pub?" Ruby asked.

"Apparently so. It was one of her favourite haunts."

"While dead and alive," Ruby said with a laugh. "Gosh! What an exciting ghost."

"Yes, if such a thing existed, she'd be fascinating to converse with. I found photographs of her. Old sepia tints. There's a striking resemblance to Millicent."

"Was Millicent receptive to a visit from us?" Ruby drove along narrow streets as we left the busy centre of London and headed to the respectable suburb of Ealing.

"She was willing to meet, although our telephone conversation was over in a matter of seconds," I said. "She's a straightforward lady, so I shall treat her as such. No dithering with small talk."

Ruby signalled a left turn. "That night at the pub, she was angry enough to kill. But aren't the police still focused on Grace and the poisoned bottle of wine? It's a crucial piece of evidence that will be hard to discount."

"While they drag their heels investigating that avenue, we may as well put ourselves to good use and ensure no one slips away unnoticed. Inspector Templeton was most unhelpful when I spoke to him and pressed for answers."

Ruby laughed again. "You'll frighten him away if you're too sharp."

"He can stay or go. It's no concern of mine."

Benji sat up and rested his head on my shoulder.

"Almost there, boy," I said.

"Benji likes Inspector Templeton," Ruby said.

"Because Inspector Templeton treats him to biscuits when he thinks I'm not looking," I retorted. "That's a simple way to this dog's heart."

"Dogs only like people of good character. Inspector Templeton has faults, but I consider him to be an excellent fellow."

I pressed my lips together and stared pointedly out of the front window. Ruby was forever attempting to matchmake me, but she wouldn't succeed in this instance.

Ten minutes later, we stopped outside a small block of flats. The outside was tidy and the paintwork was fresh. We located Millicent's flat, and I knocked on the door.

She opened it, dressed in workmen's overalls, her hair tied off her face, and a paintbrush in one hand. "Come in. I can't stop. I don't want the wall to dry patchy. I wanted to be done before you arrived." Millicent turned and marched away, leaving us with no choice but to follow her.

The air smelled of fresh paint and the acidic tang of brush cleaner. The room we entered was clearly the main living area, but the furnishings were concealed under white cloths.

"Mind your dog doesn't get paint on his fur," Millicent said. "The walls are still wet."

"He'll stay put." I gestured for Benji to sit. "Have you just moved in?"

"No, this is my older brother's place. I live closer to the Craven Arms. Got my own small flat."

"Where is your brother?" Ruby asked. "Shouldn't he be helping?"

"He's getting out of the hospital soon, so we wanted to make it nice for him. It's only our dad left, and he's too sick to do much, so it fell on my shoulders."

"I'm sorry to hear about your brother," Ruby said. "It sounds serious."

Millicent dipped her brush into a tin of cream paint and set to work on the wall. "We didn't think he'd pull through. He was one of the last out of his trench before it was overrun. Got a lungful of gas for his efforts, so he's been convalescing since the war ended. The trouble is, he's in a grand old place down in Surrey that was converted into a convalescence hospital, so I don't get to visit much."

"You must miss him," Ruby said.

"He's family. Of course I do. The doctors have done what they can for him, so they're sending him home." Millicent gestured with the brush. "He never took care of this place, but he owns it, so I wanted to surprise him and smarten it up for when he gets back."

"That's kind of you," Ruby said.

"It's the least I can do after everything he did for this country. Not that he got any thanks for it. I even had to fight to get him financial help." Millicent smashed the brush bristles against the wall. "And he can't work because of his damaged lungs. He should have run faster. Escaped the gas attack."

The use of gas in the latter part of the Great War had been roundly condemned. Many men suffered terrible ill-health as a result of its inefficient dispersal during a desperate period of fighting.

"You said you had questions about my great-grandmother?" Millicent had her back to us as she talked.

"The London Times is publishing an article about the ghost investigation held at the Craven Arms," I said. "I wanted to make sure we covered all angles."

"I didn't think a paper of that reputation would publish lies?"

"It will be a fair article," I said. "And since I was there, only the truth will be told."

"I doubt your newspaper staff knows what that word means." Millicent slapped more paint on the wall. "Go on, ask your questions."

"Before we get to your ancestor, I wanted your opinion of William Lombard."

Millicent huffed air through her nose. "Didn't like him when he was alive, still don't like him now he's dead."

"You've clashed?" Ruby asked.

"He wanted to interview me for his new book. He said there was bound to be a connection between me and my great-grandmother, and he wanted to use his power to unveil it." Millicent snorted loudly. "What a load of old tosh. The man was a charlatan. Anyone with half a brain could see he didn't know what he was doing."

"His books are popular," I said. "And I've recently learned he held private sittings for people who wished to speak to those on the other side."

"The other side of what? More fool them for parting with their money. He pocketed it and fed them whatever honeyed lies they desired. Mr Lombard was a pest, always wanting to know about my great-grandmother."

"It was clear during your argument with Nicholas at the pub that you didn't appreciate your great-grandmother's name being used," I said.

"They both knew how much I hated it, but Mr Lombard's only interest was making up lies about the dead so he could make money. It was disgusting." Millicent glanced over her shoulder at us. "I told him to leave her alone. Even if there is something else after we die, why bother the ghosts?"

"It sounds like you argued about this issue frequently," I said.

"I'd been telephoning his publisher and writing letters to let them know I disapproved of what was planned. Nicholas gave me the brush-off, so I visited the pub. And there they were, with their smug smiles and snake oil charm, conning those sad, lonely ladies. I saw red." She looked into her pot of paint and dropped the brush into it. "That's the last section I wanted to cover. If you want to know more about my great-grandmother, I can take you to her."

Ruby's eyes widened. "Surely, not her ghost?"

Millicent pressed her lips together. "Hardly. After all, if you believe the lies, she spends her time wandering around the Craven Arms scaring people. Give me five minutes to wash up, and I'll take you for a walk. She's not buried far from here."

Ruby glanced at me, and I nodded. We waited outside, since the paint fumes were strong, and I walked Benji on a patch of grass while Millicent freshened up.

"She's a plain speaker," Ruby said. "Would a killer be so honest?"

DEATH AT THE CRAVEN ARMS

"Although Grace is still our prime suspect, we can't rule Millicent out," I said. "She snuck into the pub after she'd been told to leave, so she was there at the time of the murder. We need to know more."

Millicent strode out of the main door and turned left. "Follow me. The cemetery is ten minutes from here." She set a swift pace and marched off. I had to put on a spurt to keep up with her, and Ruby was almost cantering.

We walked past more flats, small suburban houses, and a public park before arriving at a large wrought-iron gate, which Millicent pushed open. The sign on it read Ealing Cemetery.

Our feet crunched along the neat gravel path as we passed headstones, mausoleums, and a number of freshly filled graves, the earth still heaped on top.

"Because of the way my great-grandmother died, she wasn't allowed to be buried in the main part of the cemetery." Millicent left the path and headed into the longer grass. "But she was a regular churchgoer and generous to the parish."

I didn't reveal to Millicent that I'd already snooped into her ancestor's background, so simply acknowledged the information with a nod.

"The old parish priest had a soft spot for her, and, according to old family gossip, a deal was struck that my great-grandmother could be buried in a corner of the graveyard, so she'd be in consecrated ground. She has a headstone, but the only markings on it are her initials. Apparently, it was to avoid a scandal."

We passed several trees and were soon concealed from any curious onlookers. No one would see what we were doing by the time we reached a small squat lump of stone.

"Here lies great-Granny Annie." Millicent patted the top of the stone. "A force to be reckoned with."

"Your great-grandmother led a colourful life?" I asked.

"Highway robber. Dead proud of it, she was, too," Millicent said. "She looked after people who couldn't look after themselves. Of course, the law caught up with her and she was hung. That's why she was tucked away here."

"I can see why Mr Lombard was so fascinated by her," Ruby said. "She must have been an interesting woman to know."

Millicent's eyes narrowed. "I suppose the article will claim my great-grandmother came back and pushed Mr Lombard down the stairs?"

"That's not an angle I'm pursuing," I said. "And he didn't die from a fall. Have the police not updated you?"

"I've barely spoken to them. They took my statement after it happened and telephoned with a follow up question, but that was it. He didn't get drunk and fall over his own feet?"

"Mr Lombard was poisoned," I said. "Unfortunately, so was Ruby."

Millicent's mouth dropped open, and she stared first at me and then Ruby. "Blimey! Sorry. I thought it was odd when the police asked if I'd been ill after the event. I told them I was sick to my stomach having to deal with Mr Lombard, but that was it. It makes sense now."

"The police are investigating how he was poisoned," I said. "It's likely they'll want to talk to you again."

"Why me? I've got nothing to tell them. I wasn't even there. I got kicked out before the ghost hunt began." Millicent rubbed her hands against her arms.

"But you snuck back in. Benji found you."

Millicent's nose crinkled, but she didn't reply.

"Why return to the Craven Arms?" I asked. "You must have realised you wouldn't be able to stop the ghost hunt."

Millicent stared in the direction of the church. "I'm not sure why I did it. I was still angry with Mr Lombard. Maybe I thought I'd mess with his stupid investigation and make him think he'd seen a real ghost. Then he might stop messing with them. I don't know. It was silly. And a waste of time. It was pitch black, and I couldn't find anyone."

It was a foolish move, and it meant Millicent had been inside the pub at the time of the murder. Was it possible that she'd snuck open the cellar door and pushed Mr Lombard down the stairs? If she hadn't been the one to poison him, she wouldn't have known he was already dying.

Had two people attempted to murder Mr Lombard that night? Was he really so unpopular?

"It's getting cold," Millicent said. "And I need to tidy my brother's flat and clean the paint brushes before they set hard."

"Thank you for your time," I said. "We'll take a walk around, so don't wait for us."

"I expect you're hoping to see a ghost. More fool you if you are."

We walked back to the main path with Millicent, and she strode away after a curt goodbye.

"I love a cemetery." Ruby rubbed her hands together in delight. "Let's investigate the headstones while you exercise Benji. We've got time before it gets too dark and chilly."

I nodded as I followed Ruby along the path, my thoughts full of Millicent's comments. She had a motive, no alibi, and a fearsome temper. Even though poison was in the mix, and Grace the likely killer, I was still uncertain of Millicent's innocence.

"Look! It's the foundation stone laid for Annie." Ruby crouched to read the faded, weather worn words. "Annie Crophampton. A most generous benefactor."

"Even bad people do good things," I said. "Let's walk a circuit to get some air. Then you need an early night. And I have a lot to think about."

Chapter 16

Although I was focused on my work, content at my desk, editing my latest obituary, I was also observing Uncle Harry and Bob. They'd been deep in conversation in Uncle Harry's office with the door closed for ten minutes.

I repressed a sigh and resisted the urge to chew the end of my pencil. When Bob had a bee in his bonnet, he never let it go, bending poor Uncle Harry's ear until he admitted defeat. And usually, Bob's bees involved me.

I'd just finished outlining a new obituary when Uncle Harry's door opened. Bob lumbered out, giving me a filthy look before he headed to his desk.

"Benji, I fear we're about to be scolded," I whispered. He cocked an ear and whined.

"Veronica, a word," Uncle Harry called out.

"Be right with you." I grabbed my work, pasted on a smile, and headed into my uncle's office.

"Close the door and take a seat. I suppose you saw that?" Uncle Harry tipped back in his chair, lacing his fingers behind his head.

"As hard as I try, Bob is impossible to ignore. Have you noticed how he wheezes when he walks? I'd say it was because he'd had a lungful of mustard gas, but we all know he didn't serve. I blame the wheezing on his liking for fried egg sandwiches."

"He couldn't serve because he has flat feet and is missing half a lung. No picking on Bob. The man works hard, so he's allowed his fried egg indulgences."

"If his dreadful diet continues, he'll give himself a heart attack," I said.

A smile flickered across Uncle Harry's tired looking face. "Imagine that. You'd get to write his obituary. Would there be any kind words for poor old Robert?"

"You make me sound like a monster! If pressed, I could find one or two good things to say about him. Let me think." I steepled my fingers and set my expression to pensive.

"Don't joke about Bob. As usual, he's not happy with you."

"What's he been tattling about this time?" I asked.

"It's not just him. I've been speaking to my contacts at the police station. I know all about the poisoning." Uncle Harry blew out a breath. "It's lucky you weren't poisoned, just like Ruby."

"It was unfortunate Ruby got caught in the crossfire," I said. "But she's made a remarkable recovery."

"In the wrong dose, strychnine is nasty. Although there are still doctors who prescribe it in certain tonics, but I'm not sure it does people any good."

"Mr Lombard's dose was high enough for the police to be certain it wasn't from a prescribed tonic."

Uncle Harry leaned back even more, a twinkle of amusement in his eyes. Sometimes, he looked so like my late father, it made my heart ache. "When Bob learned

Ruby got a dose of poison too, he said that would never have happened to his wife. She wouldn't have been permitted out late at night, drinking on her own."

I raised my eyebrows. "I didn't think Bob was married."

"He was speaking hypothetically."

"Does he even know what that word means?" I sighed as Uncle Harry glowered at me. "I was never at risk. You knew I was visiting the Craven Arms for a story. What was I supposed to do? Ignore a family's business concern because it's not deemed appropriate by a handful of stuffy sorts who think we're still in the Victorian era? Women have rights and freedom."

"Don't get on your soapbox," Uncle Harry said. "I'm always on your side."

"Perhaps not this time?"

He sighed. "Bob has a point. I send you to report on stories, and I forget you're a single woman. Times are changing, but there are still standards and expectations. I don't want your work to hinder your happiness."

I narrowed my eyes. "Are you suggesting because I'm a working woman with a degree of independence, I'll be unable to catch a suitable husband? If that's what you think my only ambition is in life, and my only source of happiness, then you don't know me at all."

"None of that sharp talk. You're a clever thing, and the right gentleman will appreciate that." Uncle Harry sat forward and rubbed his forehead. "Step back from this story. It'll make both of our lives easier."

As tempting as it was to dig in my heels and argue my corner, I tossed an olive branch. "I know I'll have no opportunity to write the full story on what happened at the Craven Arms, but I intend to write Mr Lombard's obituary. And my mother has a copy of his latest book, so I'm well-versed in all things ghostly."

Uncle Harry softly groaned his displeasure. "Keep ghostly killers out of the obituary. And do your level best to be pleasant to Bob. He's been talking to the other fellows, stirring trouble for you."

"You want me to be pleasant to a man who's trying to lose me my job?"

Uncle Harry closed his eyes for a few seconds. "If you can't be civil, then stay out of his way."

"It's always my intention." I leaned over the desk and gave Uncle Harry my work. "For you to check. I'll have more later."

"That's my girl. You always come through with the goods. Make sure you look suitably scolded, so Bob leaves me alone for the rest of the day, or he'll charge back in here and start yelling."

As hard as it was to muster a pitiful expression, I wouldn't let Uncle Harry down, so I slouched my shoulders as I returned to my desk. The second I sat down, the telephone rang. I picked it up.

"Veronica, it's Inspector Templeton."

"Do you have good news?" I asked.

"We have progress. The tests are back. Strychnine was found in the bottle of wine Grace left for Mr Lombard. We're bringing her in."

I sighed in relief and sank into my seat. "That's excellent news. I'm sure you'll do a thorough job. But don't forget, there are still many—"

"No! I don't need any more complications. As I've told you before, I know how to do my job."

"If you'd allow me to finish speaking before butting in, I wanted to remind you there are other suspects. I spoke to Millicent yesterday."

It sounded as if Inspector Templeton was ripping paper. "Now you think she poisoned Mr Lombard and not Grace? Even though Grace was seen handing over the bottle of poisoned wine?"

"I didn't say that exactly. What's Grace's motive?" I asked.

"She discovered Mr Lombard was a fraud and grew angry with him. She'd invested time in his falsehoods. Now we have evidence of where the poison came from, the motive is secondary. We know he drank the wine, and so did Ruby, so we've got Grace bang to rights."

I hesitated. "It does sound like it."

"Good. Now, it's time you left this case alone. Focus on your work, and we'll have Grace charged before the end of the week. If she confesses during questioning, so much the better."

Although the evidence pointed to Grace, I felt a certain amount of untidy business was still leftover.

"You scare me when you go silent," Inspector Templeton said. "Are we clear? No more snooping. The case is as good as solved."

"Whatever you think, Inspector," I said.

"You're ... agreeing with me?"

"I'm busy. Let me know at your earliest convenience what happens with Grace."

We said our goodbyes, and I hung up the telephone. Was I overcomplicating things? There were other motives and opportunities, but perhaps the mystery had been solved.

I shook my head. Until I was certain, and despite Uncle Harry and Inspector Templeton telling me I shouldn't, I wouldn't stop looking into Mr Lombard's murder.

The evening took me, Ruby, and Benji back to the Craven Arms. I was delighted to find it busy. A bustling pub meant excellent profits. We even had to wait at the bar for several minutes before Joe became free.

He strode over with a big smile on his face. "I'm pleased to see you back on your feet, Miss Ruby. I've been keeping you in my thoughts."

"That's sweet of you," Ruby said. "It was my fault I was poisoned."

"I was the one who offered you the glass of wine," Joe said. "I was showing off. I was impressed by the vintage and wanted to show you I knew all about fancy wines. I'm glad you only had a sip. I'd have thrown myself into the Thames if you hadn't pulled through."

Ruby patted his hand. "I deliberately made myself better as quickly as possible so you wouldn't worry unnecessarily."

Joe grinned. "Same as always?"

"Sadly, I'm not drinking at the moment, under doctor's orders," Ruby said glumly. "I'll have a small orange juice."

I stuck with Ruby and ordered the same. "It's busy tonight."

"The extra trade caught me by surprise," Joe said as he gave us our drinks. "Everyone's here because they want to see the new ghost. The talk is all about the murder, and the punters expect Mr Lombard to float up from the cellar and give them a scare."

"Have you had any new ghostly encounters while changing the barrels?" I asked, pretending to be shocked.

"I've not seen the old ghosts or the new ghosts." Joe tapped his nose. "But don't tell the public that. I don't want them disappointed."

"We'll keep it between us," I said. "The police have someone in custody for Mr Lombard's murder."

"That's grand news." Joe's smile faded. "You don't seem happy about it."

"Veronica thinks there are too many loose ends," Ruby said. "We're here to recreate the evening and see if we can find any holes. Or should that be untied pieces of thread to pull on?"

"Don't mind me. Poke around all you like. If I can be of any help, just shout." Joe was called away by a customer.

"There's Reverend Worthington." Ruby pointed across the pub.

We walked over to the table he sat at and greeted him. He had a small sweet sherry in front of him, and was sitting alone, reading a newspaper.

He greeted us cordially. "Are you ladies here for another ghostly adventure?"

"One evening of ghosts was quite enough for us," I said.

"It's such a shock, what happened. I've been praying for William. Although I told him he shouldn't tamper with the unknown, he didn't listen, and this tragedy struck."

"Are you unaware of the cause of death?" I asked.

"A fall, wasn't it?" Reverend Worthington blinked at me owlishly. "I briefly spoke to the police that evening, but I had no helpful information. And they contacted me to see if I had been unwell. That was unusual, but I suppose some people have unpleasant symptoms due to shock."

"The police discovered Mr Lombard didn't die from a fall, accidental or deliberate," I said. "He had poison in his system."

"Oh, my!" Reverend Worthington placed a hand against his chest. "He was murdered?"

"It seems so. How well did you know him?" I asked.

"Not at all. He wasn't a man of my parish. I believe he travelled extensively for work. I don't know where he lived, though. What a dreadful business. It was definitely poison?"

"No doubt about it," I said.

"Well, I shall continue to pray for his soul. I didn't agree with his obsession with the other side, but that's a wicked thing to do to a man." Reverend Worthington finished his sweet sherry in a single gulp, then pulled out a tin of peppermints and popped one into his mouth.

We said our goodbyes and walked through the pub, discussing how the room had been laid out on the evening of the ghost hunt. It was hard to get a clear view of everything because the place was crowded, so we returned to the bar.

"Joe, could we have a word?" I asked.

He dashed over, a piece of pork scratching in his hand for Benji. "Did you figure things out? The police have the right person?"

"I'm yet to be convinced. What did you do with Mr Lombard's bottle of wine after you opened it?"

"I showed it to him, and he was pleased. He said it was his favourite, and he'd drink some later. I uncorked the bottle and left it to breathe."

"Where did you put the open bottle?" I asked.

"I tucked it under the bar counter. It's good to let red wine breathe before drinking it." Joe beamed at Ruby, always keen to impress her.

I leaned over the bar as far as I could and reached around. "It would have been easy for someone to grab the bottle."

"Why would they do that?" Joe asked.

Ruby gasped. "To add poison to it? You're thinking it wasn't Grace?"

"If someone had come to the evening with the intention of murdering Mr Lombard, they could have brought strychnine with them in the hopes of finding a way to sneak it into something he ate or drank," I said.

"I didn't watch the bottle closely," Joe said. "I was more interested in the fun and games with the ghosts. And then there was the young lady who got into a fight. There were so many distractions that night."

"Which presented opportunities for someone to add poison to the bottle of wine after you opened it," I said. "How long did it sit before you poured it?"

"A good while. I can't say for sure." Joe rubbed the back of his neck. "I never thought to keep an eye on it."

"There would have been no reason for you to. It should have been safe. How much of the wine did Mr Lombard drink?" I asked.

"He had most of the bottle. I poured Ruby a tiny glass, so Mr Lombard wouldn't notice any was missing," Joe said.

"And I'm thankful you did." Ruby squeezed my arm. "With this information, it throws everything in the air. Anyone at the ghost hunt could have added the strychnine to the wine."

"Unfortunately, it does," I said. "It's possible Grace is innocent."

Chapter 17

"You look weary. Still lovely, but there are few of us who can style out bags under their eyes. Have another cup of tea." Ruby lifted a flower-patterned teapot off the small table in a new cafe we were trying, close to home. It had opened a week ago and was charmingly called the *Thames Tea Cosy*, and it not only sold delicious food but had displays of hand-knitted teapot warmers available for purchase.

"I barely slept last night after we discovered anyone could have tampered with the wine before the lights went out in the Craven Arms." I added milk to my freshened tea and stirred it. "If there are no eyewitnesses, how will we uncover who actually poisoned Mr Lombard?"

"We should ask the pub's ghosts."

My expression soured.

"You are in a grump. Perhaps the police have it solved, and it was Grace all along. They do sometimes get things right." Ruby's hand hovered over the plate of delicate cakes we'd been presented with, along with delicious plates of scrambled eggs, bacon, and toast.

"Perhaps." I sipped my tea. I'd treated Ruby to a well-deserved brunch in an effort to ensure she forgot about her unfortunate poisoning incident. I hadn't been responsible, but it had happened in my pub, so I felt a touch guilty. "Sometimes, it is the most obvious suspect. But with so many players in the game, it would be remiss of us to dismiss the other suspects without being thorough."

"You're nothing but that. But if not Grace, then who did it?" Ruby finally selected a tiny chocolate cake with a swirl of fresh cream sandwiched in the middle and placed it on her plate. A strawberry tart followed.

"Nobody has been ruled out. And they all have excellent motives. I can't get Nicholas out of my head. From the moment he contacted me and explained the book tour, I was uncomfortable about the situation."

"Because you don't believe in ghosts," Ruby said.

"Partly that, but I wasn't comfortable with how he exploits people's grief to make money."

"Not everyone who wants to reach out to the dead is grieving," Ruby said. "Some may need information about a missing will or where the dead person left their car keys. Or they need to know the safe combination!"

"Please don't indulge the ghost fantasy any further," I said. "I understand the need to make one's fortune, but surely, there'd be better books to write and publish. Books that help people rather than scandalise a tragic situation. Nicholas is ruthless. And I fear little would stop him if he ran into a problem and grew concerned his cash cow was about to dry up."

"He wasn't pleasant when we were at the Craven Arms. There was no sadness over Mr Lombard's death, and barely a hint of shock." Ruby seemed to have forgotten her scrambled eggs in favour of more cake.

"His thoughts turned to how he could flip the death to his financial advantage. Have us claim a ghost killed Mr Lombard to ensure more copies of the book sold. It was distasteful. A man with such a cold heart could be driven to do anything if he knew he'd reap the benefits."

"We should speak to him again."

I grimaced. "I don't enjoy his company."

"Don't ask me to flirt with him to get information. I find Nicholas as oily as that kipper on the next table." Ruby inclined her head at the table occupied by an elderly gent intent on de-boning his pungent treat.

I half smiled. "I wouldn't force that punishment on you."

"I still favour Grace. The money she's been withdrawing could be at the bottom of this puzzle," Ruby said. "She's not living expensively. She didn't have on designer shoes, or carry an expensive handbag, and her clothing was several seasons past best. And I don't think she wore a jot of make-up. Could she have spent the money on Mr Lombard?"

"We know he conducted private sittings with her," I said, "but I can't imagine those would have been extortionate. How else would he have gotten money out of her? What service did he provide that caused her to fall into debt?"

Ruby was temporarily dazzled as a small dessert cart was pushed past our table. She sighed. "The doctor insisted I eat plain food."

"Then we shouldn't be eating any of this," I said. "I'll ask the server to take our brunch and bring you dry toast."

"Don't you dare! My stomach is perfectly fine." Ruby's stomach gurgled as if suggesting it wasn't quite itself. She rested a hand on her belly. "We'll have a plain dinner."

"Boiled potatoes and green vegetables for you after this indulgence. I don't want you having a setback and ending up in the hospital again."

"A small bout of poisoning won't slow me. And I want this case solved. I need to know who almost ended my life."

"So do I. I won't rest easy until the rotter is behind bars."

We took a few moments from our sleuthing to enjoy our brunch. The eggs were perfect, and the buttered toast deliciously crunchy.

"This may help." Ruby reached into her oversized handbag and pulled out a copy of Mr Lombard's book. "I borrowed it from your mother. She said she was up late reading it every night. It's turned her into a believer."

I glared at the book. "If we're not careful, she'll start believing our house is haunted and have the neighbours around to hunt for cold spots and hold hands while they summon the spirits."

Ruby bit her bottom lip. "She briefly mentioned trying to contact your father."

I hid my face in my hands and peeked through my fingers. "I hope you talked her out of it."

"It was a passing comment, but the book has got her thinking." Ruby hesitated, her expression pensive. "I know we don't talk about what happened to him, but you must still have questions."

My appetite vanished. My beloved father, Davey Vale, was never far from my thoughts, and it was a mystery as to why he went to Beachy Head. It was a notorious spot where people took their own lives, and although the police never found his body, there were personal effects left behind. As sad as it was, I refused to dwell on something I couldn't change. Focusing on the past led to maudlin feelings. But in the quiet of night, after a long day and trying conversations with my mother, I longed for my father to still be here. He'd had a way of making anyone smile.

"If a seance is mentioned again, change the subject," I said. "We don't need to enter those murky waters. Mother's been doing so well since you moved in. She's been getting out of bed every day!"

"I'm glad I'm such an excellent influence," Ruby said. "Next thing, I'll be getting Matthew out in the fresh air. He's so pale. He worries me."

"Matthew has his struggles. He's doing better, though. The puppy has lifted his spirits."

"I can see why. Such an adorable creature. Will you keep him?"

"It's a possibility. And Benji likes him." Benji was currently at home with the pup, teaching him the delicate art of not urinating on people's shoes.

"They're a perfect match. And once Matthew has his own dog, he'll have to leave the house to walk him."

"That's an excellent point. I shall encourage the adoption." Ruby had such a generous heart, always thinking of others, providing there wasn't cake or new handbags to distract her. "And my mother considers you a part of the family. So do I. She will always want to look after you."

"I feel the same. With my parents so often away, you're my second family."

"And family helps each other. Which is why we must reveal who poisoned you," I said.

Ruby turned over Mr Lombard's book and opened the back page. "We need to be clear on Grace's motive."

"What are you thinking?" I asked. "It's the weekend, so we have all day to explore possibilities, but I don't want you overdoing things."

"Once we've consumed this delicious food, I'll need to spend the day on my feet. I can't afford new dresses, so I have to squeeze into the ragged old things I've got, and I won't be able to do that if I gain an ounce."

I shook my head in fond exasperation. Ruby had an exquisite wardrobe and spent every penny on the latest fashions.

"This is what I'm thinking." Ruby tapped a finger on the open book. "There's a postal address in here. Anyone interested in a private reading or a consultation with Mr Lombard wrote to him and he replied by return of post. It's a north London address, so not too far out of our way."

"Excellent work. We'll go directly to the address and see if anyone is home."

As tempting as it was to linger over a long brunch and gossip with Ruby, we had the business of murder to attend to. Once the bill was paid, we left the delightful cafe and drove to an address in Hampstead, North London. It took some searching, but we found a small gold plaque in an alleyway with William Lombard's name engraved on it.

"I see someone moving around inside." Ruby peered through the window next to the door. "That's a stroke of luck."

I knocked at the door. We were ignored for several minutes, until it was finally opened by a sad looking, slightly disheveled middle-aged woman with graying hair, dressed in a dour brown suit.

"We're not open for business," she said by way of a welcome.

I made the introductions. "We are sorry to bother you at the weekend, but we were two of the last people to see Mr Lombard alive."

The woman blinked at us several times. "You were at the Craven Arms?"

I nodded. "My family owns the pub. And I also write for the London Times. I'm gathering information about Mr Lombard for an article and his obituary. It sounds like he led a fascinating life."

"I should say he did. And he's left it all behind for me to pack up." The woman heaved a sigh. "I'm Sylvia Brewster. I was his secretary. I looked after the letters and telephone calls. Basically kept him organised. Well, as much as I could. He wasn't an easy man to keep on track."

"I'm terribly sorry for your loss," Ruby said. "Had you worked for him long?"

"Going on three years. In the ghost business, you understand. I knew him before that when he was in sales. I worked for a publishing house that printed Bibles. We got friendly when he used to come into the office," Sylvia said. "One day, he said he was starting his own business and did I want to join him?"

"You're a believer in ghosts?" I asked.

"No. But I was bored, and my former boss was a drunk and used to yell at everyone. What Mr Lombard had planned sounded interesting. Odd, and I can't say I've ever seen a ghost, but it made for a change. And the money was better."

"Would you mind if we came in and asked you some questions?" I said.

Sylvia hesitated. "I have a lot to do, so I can only spare a few minutes. But it would be good to talk about him. He always made me smile with his ghost stories." She held the door open wider and allowed us into a small narrow corridor with two rooms, one on either side.

Sylvia pushed open the door to the right. "This one is almost empty. It was Mr Lombard's room. He travelled a lot, so he didn't need much space, but he'd sometimes work here, usually on his books. My room is the one opposite. That's where I'm tidying." She led us into the other room. It was a clutter of boxes, paperwork, and stationery.

The telephone on the desk rang.

"Excuse me. That'll be another unhappy client. I wrote to everyone who had an appointment to ensure they knew they would no longer be able to see Mr Lombard. Well, not unless he visited them as a ghost." She barked a short laugh and picked up the telephone.

"I wonder if the police have been here yet?" Ruby murmured to me.

"With their efforts focused on Grace, I doubt Inspector Templeton is interested in pulling apart this office," I said. "Although he does a reasonable job of looking into backgrounds, this is the first I've learned of Mr Lombard having an office in town. If the police didn't dig deeply enough, they could have missed this."

"I'm sorry. There's nothing I can do to bring him back," Sylvia said sharply. "And all deposits are nonrefundable." She was quiet for a few seconds. "If you're such a firm believer, make contact with Mr Lombard on the other side. I'm sure he'll help. Goodbye."

"As you predicted?" I asked.

Sylvia sighed as she set down the telephone. "I've been getting calls since word got out. People are ever so cross. But it's not my fault a ghost did him in."

"Is that what you think happened to him?" I asked.

Sylvia piled books into a box. "That's what his fancy publisher said. Mr Hawthorn came by yesterday and told me to get rid of everything. I'm to send any relevant paperwork and books to him, but the rest can be thrown away."

"Nicholas was here?"

"He'd often stop by when Mr Lombard was in town to see how his writing was going. Not that he'd written much lately. His private client work made him plenty of money."

"It sounds like that side of the business was popular," I said.

"I should say it was. The telephone was always ringing. And I must have had twenty letters to deal with every day from people asking to make contact with those on the other side."

"Was that the only service he offered?" Ruby asked.

"No. He'd expanded his area of expertise." Sylvia didn't fail to hide a brief smirk. "Many clients wanted him to visit because they were concerned about a haunting. Others wanted private sittings, or to go on an immersive experience."

"What would an immersive experience entail?" I asked.

"Just that. He'd take a client on a haunted retreat for a week to communicate with ghosts."

"That sounds intense," Ruby said. "What did they do at these retreats?"

Sylvia stopped sorting through a pile of books. "I had the misfortune to go on one. Mr Lombard said it would be a good experience, so I could tell potential clients how incredible it was. He'd hire an entire house in the middle of nowhere. He always picked one that was supposed to be haunted so the spirits would come through and talk."

"Did you ever hear any ghosts speak to him?" Ruby grew wide-eyed as she listened to the far-fetched tale.

"Never heard so much as an impolite burp. I travelled with him down to Kent, and we spent a week in a cold, creepy place with no proper wiring and freezing drafts, with this broken-hearted old woman who wanted to talk to her husband," Sylvia said. "She said he'd left her money, and she wanted to thank him and learn the combination to the house safe. Silly old bugger wasn't organised with the paperwork, so she couldn't get her hands on her jewels!"

"What happened while you were there?" I asked.

"I caught a cold. But the old lady went away happy. I didn't see everything that went on, because Mr Lombard held closed-room events, where it was just the two of them communicating with the spirits. He'd light candles and waft around strange-smelling herbs. It was all very atmospheric, but I never understood why burning herbs would summon a ghost."

"Do you know if a client called Grace Vilein ever went on an immersive experience?" I asked.

Sylvia smiled. "I know Grace. She used to visit twice a week and have private sessions. She was devoted to Mr Lombard. Grace is a sweet lady, but far too naïve."

"And the immersive retreats?"

"She went on three. I asked her once if she thought they were worth it because they were ever such a lot of money, but Grace thought Mr Lombard was wonderful. She never had a bad word to say about him and always came back from the retreats happy she'd been able to speak to the only person who understood her. At least, that's what she told me."

I pressed my lips together. This was bad news for Grace. If she'd discovered Mr Lombard was conning her out of a substantial sum of money to attend sham spirit summoning events, it was an excellent motive for murder.

"Why do you want to know about the clients?" Sylvia's gaze narrowed. "Are you contacting them for further information for your article?"

"We want a full picture of Mr Lombard's life," I said. "His client work was important to him."

Sylvia shrugged. "Whatever you say. I should get on. Mr Hawthorn wants this place cleared by the end of the week."

We thanked Sylvia for her time and left the office.

"Grace went into debt to pay for these fraudulent ghostly retreats," Ruby said.

I nodded. "She was desperate to speak to her grandmother and thought Mr Lombard would help. No matter how much it cost, she was determined to make contact with her."

"From all accounts, it sounds like she did. But if Grace was so pleased with Mr Lombard's work, why did she poison him?"

"What if something went wrong at the last retreat?" I asked.

"Grace discovered Mr Lombard was pulling the wool over her eyes, so got revenge?"

"It's a possible motive. Before we focus solely on Grace, I have another avenue to pursue."

Ruby's eyes sparkled with excitement. "Who do we question next?"

"How would you like drinks at the Savoy?"

Chapter 18

Fortunately, we were too full from brunch to need to order from the Savoy's luncheon menu, which meant I didn't have to spend a week's wages to dine. I was content to sit, sipping my gin fizz, while Ruby glumly had another orange juice.

"This is where Mr Lombard and Nicholas would often come," I said. "If they were regulars, they could have been noticed by the wait staff."

Ruby gazed around with delighted satisfaction at the busy restaurant, dazzled by the expensive refinement. The Savoy attracted a certain type of person. Individuals who enjoyed overt displays of wealth and didn't think twice about ordering a second bottle of champagne with their lunch, while they dined under crystal chandeliers.

"If someone brought me here, I'd be won over to whatever scheme they had planned," Ruby said. "It's so enchanting."

"The prices do not enchant," I said.

"We should save up and treat ourselves," Ruby suggested. "We deserve more than a swift drink at the bar."

"The people serving behind the bar are often the most observant." I gestured to the smartly dressed dark-haired bartender who had presented us with our drinks.

"Are you ready for more?" he was swift to enquire.

"We would like information," I said. "How long have you worked here?"

"Four years." His gaze was curious. "What information would you ladies like? I can tell you the best tourist places to visit if you're not local."

"We're Londoners, born and bred," I said. "I'm looking for information about a customer who came here regularly. Nicholas Hawthorn."

The bartender took a step back. "I'm sorry, but we don't gossip about our regulars. People come here because they appreciate discretion."

"You do know him?"

"I really couldn't say."

I slid money out of my handbag and set it on the bar. "Is there nothing I can do to help you recall anything useful?"

He smiled, and the money disappeared. "Mr Hawthorn works in publishing. He often brings clients here when he wants to impress them."

"Being brought here would impress me," Ruby said.

The bartender grinned, relaxing now he'd received his hefty tip. "We do get the more refined gentlemen bringing their lady friends here, and they always seem thrilled. I'm sure if you ask your gentleman friend, he'd treat you to a meal."

"We're perfectly capable of treating ourselves," I said.

DEATH AT THE CRAVEN ARMS

The bartender's gaze turned appraising. "It's always a pleasure to meet independent women. Are you in the publishing business, too?"

"After a fashion. Newspapers," I said.

"Horses for me," Ruby added.

"Getting back to Mr Hawthorn and his clients, did you ever see him entertain an author called William Lombard?"

"Yes. They'd dine here at least once a month."

"Did you overhear their conversations?"

"I stay behind the bar. This is my domain," the bartender said. "But it's funny you should ask. The last time they dined together, they didn't look happy. Mr Hawthorn spent a lot of time glowering at Mr Lombard. Usually, their lunches are full of expensive bottles of red wine and laughter. Not that last luncheon, though."

"Did any of the waiters overhear their argument?" I asked.

"They're as discreet as me. Although I'm sure, with the right incentive, they could be encouraged to talk." He made the universal sign for money with his fingers.

"This is a matter of some urgency," I said. "It seems you're not aware that Mr Lombard died recently."

"And his death wasn't an accident." There was a touch of drama in Ruby's tone.

"That's news to me! Let me see what I can do." The bartender hurried away, and we were left to enjoy the murmur of polite conversation and the clink of cutlery on china plates.

"It seems you're on to something," Ruby said. "If Mr Lombard and Nicholas were butting heads, Nicholas would have wanted him gone."

"And found a way to do it that would maximise the return on his investment." My nose wrinkled at the distasteful possibility.

The bartender returned a few moments later with a fresh-faced waiter in tow. "This is Robert. He looks after Mr Hawthorn when he dines with us. These nice ladies have something to ask you."

Robert looked hesitant until I tipped him generously. He tilted an imaginary hat. "What can I do for you?"

"We're interested in the last time you served Mr Hawthorn and his client, William Lombard."

"I remember the meal. It wasn't enjoyable to serve them. Is Mr Lombard really dead?"

"He is. He perished in a London pub during a ghost hunt."

Robert glanced at the bartender. "And it wasn't an accident?"

"I can confirm it wasn't. Could you tell us what you overheard the two men talking about the last time they dined here?"

Robert considered the question. "They were arguing over a book. Mr Hawthorn kept saying he needed a date, and he refused to be kept waiting any longer."

"We know Mr Lombard was late in delivering his new book," Ruby said.

Robert nodded. "Mr Lombard kept talking about the spirits not aligning, and Mr Hawthorn was dismissing him, telling him not to talk nonsense, and the public expected the book."

"Was there a resolution to their argument?" I asked.

"Of sorts, but I doubt it was one either was happy with," Robert said. "Not long after I served their main course, I checked their table to make sure everything was to their liking. They barely acknowledged me, since they were glaring at each other. As I walked away, Mr Hawthorn threatened Mr Lombard."

My eyebrows rose. "What was the threat?"

Robert glanced around. "He said Mr Lombard was easy to replace, and his fans would forget him when they met a more accomplished liar."

"How did Mr Lombard respond?"

"He said something about being insulted and he wouldn't stand for it. He was the expert, and no one would ever replace him. Mr Lombard threw down his napkin and walked out of the restaurant."

"And he didn't return?"

"Mr Hawthorn finished his meal alone and drank an entire bottle of vintage red to himself." Robert looked over at his tables. "I must get back. I hope that was useful."

"Thank you, most useful," I murmured.

The bartender also left us to serve other customers.

"This is a turn-up," Ruby said. "Mr Lombard and Nicholas were no longer on friendly terms."

"And Nicholas has found a replacement," I said. "When I visited his office, George Cloister was just arriving as I left. He's the new ghost hunter extraordinaire Nicholas plans to promote."

"What if Mr Lombard figured out what was going on and refused to go quietly?" Ruby asked.

"Mr Cloister and Nicholas would have been stuck," I said. "They had a plan to move forward with new books, but if Mr Lombard refused to leave his contract, trouble would have brewed. Perhaps Nicholas couldn't afford to take on both authors."

"But with one dead, it solves the problem," Ruby said.

"And if they worked together at the Craven Arms, it would have been simple for one of them to slip the poison into the opened bottle of wine. Perhaps it was Mr Cloister, and Nicholas caused a distraction." I mulled over the possibility. "Nicholas could have watched Mr Lombard requesting a bottle of red wine before the event began."

"He must have considered it a stroke of luck when Grace handed the wine to Joe. Nicholas was gifted a perfect opportunity," Ruby said.

"And gifted the perfect person to frame," I said. "All he had to do was wait for the right moment."

"Nicholas and Mr Cloister had an opportunity, a motive, and no decent alibis!"

"The same as everyone else," I mused, exasperation flickering inside me. "Why must there be so many credible suspects? Will there ever be a case when it's simply one victim and one killer, with the murder weapon still in their hand?"

"Where's the fun in that?" Ruby smiled at me. "If you weren't presented with a challenge, you'd grow bored. And you're a frightful nuisance when you're bored."

"How well you know me. Let's finish our drinks, then we need to inform Inspector Templeton he has the wrong woman."

Chapter 19

It was after six o'clock by the time we'd weaved our way back into London to speak to Inspector Templeton about Grace's innocence.

I announced us at the police station's front desk, and we were told to take a seat. We'd been sitting for fifteen frustrating minutes, and there was still no sign of Inspector Templeton.

"Don't tell me he's avoiding you again," Ruby said. "He must know we're here because of the murder investigation."

"He'd better not be in the process of charging Grace," I said. "It's too soon. As we're still discovering, the other suspects are more than credible."

Five more minutes of waiting, and I'd had enough of the uncomfortable seats and lack of communication. I returned to the desk. "It really is important we see Inspector Templeton. It's regarding new information about a murder investigation. He'll want to hear this. Did you tell him why we're here?"

"I've been to check on him, miss," the police officer said. "He's interviewing someone. He can't be disturbed."

"Is he interviewing Grace Vilein?"

His eyebrows lifted. "I can't say. Would you like me to bring you both a cup of tea? Or perhaps you could come back tomorrow?"

"No tea. And we'll continue waiting. Let us know the moment he's out of his interview."

The police officer looked at me curiously before nodding. "Did you say your name was Veronica Vale?"

"That's me. And this is my companion, Ruby Smythe. Would you like me to write the names down?"

He grinned. "You're the one."

"The one what?"

"We've got a wager on in the office. Why don't you give me insider information so I win?"

Ruby joined me at the desk, a smile shuffling across her lips. "What's the wager about?"

"When Inspector Templeton will finally work up the courage to take your friend on a date. He's always talking about her."

An unwelcome heat crept up my neck. "We work together. Well, I unofficially volunteer to be his assistant, and he usually accepts my advice. We're best described as colleagues who work in different places. Maybe friends. Nothing more."

"What does Inspector Templeton say about Veronica?" Ruby leaned over the desk. "I'm convinced they're perfect for each other."

"That's quite enough of that," I said. "We don't want to put ideas into anyone's head. And cancel the wager. There'll be no romantic assignations between Inspector Templeton and me, so everyone will lose."

The officer looked disappointed. "If you arrange a date by the end of next month, that works for me. I could do with winning the stake."

"I'll see what we can do," Ruby stage-whispered, a gleeful look in her eyes as I dragged her back to the seats. "How exciting. After all this time, he's finally doing something about his feelings towards you."

"Inspector Templeton's feelings towards me involve irritation and frustration. That's a dreadful basis for any relationship."

"You seem to be doing well so far." Ruby tapped me on the arm. "There he is!"

Inspector Templeton passed the main door with several other people. I hopped up, dashed over, and thumped on the glass as I called out his name.

He reappeared a few seconds later, eyebrows raised, his expression set to stern.

"We need to see you about Grace, to ensure you do nothing foolish. Would you let us in?" I asked.

The officer behind the reception desk chortled at Inspector Templeton's surprised expression.

I ignored his poorly timed mirth. "This is important. Please say you haven't charged her with Mr Lombard's murder."

After a glowering look, Inspector Templeton opened the door. "As you can see, I'm busy. Grace is being taken to a cell."

I propped my hip against the door so he couldn't close it. "Has she confessed?"

"No, but we have enough evidence to charge her," Inspector Templeton replied.

Ruby hurried over and joined us. "We think you're wrong."

He took a step back. "I beg your pardon?"

"We've been asking around. Doing some more digging," I said.

"Poking about in things that don't concern you, do you mean?"

"You've already said you'd accept me poking about in this case, especially since Ruby was a victim. We have a theory about Nicholas and Mr Cloister working together. Have you considered they could be in cahoots?"

He shook his head. "Come back when you have facts. Theories give me nothing concrete to work with. We know how Mr Lombard died, and we have the poison in the wine bottle Grace gifted him. That's solid information."

"You need to go back and speak to Joe again," I said. "He uncorked the wine and left it unattended behind the bar. Anyone could have tampered with it."

"And we think Nicholas and Mr Cloister formed a partnership," Ruby said. "Mr Cloister is replacing Mr Lombard as the publisher's top ghost expert. It would have been easy for one of them to cause a distraction while the other slipped the poison into the wine."

"Did anyone see this dangerous duo working together?" Inspector Templeton sounded extremely unconvinced.

"They may have. Which is why you need to re-interview everybody," I said. "Perhaps someone in the pub saw them lurking around the bar and waiting for an opportunity to strike."

"That's not enough for me to go on," Inspector Templeton said. "We've got our woman. Grace is a lonely spinster who lives in a fantasy to cope with a less than ideal reality."

"There's nothing wrong with having a healthy imagination," I said.

"There is a line, though. Grace has crossed it. A search of her bedroom came up with a journal full of newspaper clippings and photographs of Mr Lombard. She was obsessed with him."

"If you ask me, it's unnatural," the police officer behind the desk said. "Old spinsters chasing around after famous types, thinking they'd be of interest to them. If she was married, she wouldn't behave like that."

I slid him an acerbic look. "Marriage doesn't solve everything. It often causes more problems for women when saddled with an inappropriate man."

"I doubt there were any married women at the pub that night," he said. "They were at home, looking after their families, as is only right."

"Did you dig this gentleman up from the stone age?" I asked Inspector Templeton.

"That's enough, officer," Inspector Templeton said, his attention returning to me. "What we have here is a simple case of an obsessed fan going too far. We're confirming the motive, but it appears Grace spent her money on events Mr Lombard held—going to ghost hunts, having private sittings, even going with him to isolated locations that were supposed to be haunted."

"You've learned about the immersive ghost experiences?" I asked.

"Veronica! My investigations are always thorough. Mr Lombard and his ghosts were Grace's only passions."

I tilted my head. "Has she said what went wrong between them?"

"Not as yet. But Grace had a private sitting with Mr Lombard two weeks before the ghost hunt at the Craven Arms. He must have made a mistake, or said something to offend her."

"Has Grace told you how she got the strychnine?" Ruby asked.

Inspector Templeton sighed. "It's easy to get hold of. It's a common base for rat poison."

"Has rat poison been found at her home?" I asked.

"She's not a foolish woman, just naïve. She wouldn't have left the poison tucked under her bed. Unlike the journal full of newspaper clippings." Inspector Templeton looked along the corridor. "I must go. It's late, and I have other cases to attend to. We've got the killer. You can rest easy."

I considered launching another defense for Grace's innocence, but it would fall on deaf ears. Once Inspector Templeton made a decision, there was little I could do to change his mind. But I wasn't giving up. I glared at Inspector Templeton. He glared back. The man was not budging.

"We should call it a night." Ruby gently tugged on my elbow.

Inspector Templeton broke eye contact. "Where's Benji?"

"At home with my mother. He's puppy training."

"Then you should be there, too. I'm sure he's pining for you."

The wretched fellow had just found my weak spot. I was missing Benji. As much as I didn't want to leave, there was little else to do. We bid Inspector Templeton good night and left the station.

"I despise this ending," I said as we walked to Ruby's car. "What went so badly wrong between Mr Lombard and Grace? He provided her with a source of much-needed comfort. Even if she realised, he told her untruths now and again, she could have overlooked it."

"I don't often agree with Inspector Templeton, but perhaps he's right," Ruby said. "Grace was paying to be sold a pack of lies. Whatever happened between them, she must have figured out she'd been deceived. It made her angry enough to hurt the man she adored."

We settled in the car, and I stared out of the front window, paying no attention to the passing traffic. "Mr Cloister said he was local to the Craven Arms."

"That's right," Ruby said. "He rather uncouthly said he lived within spitting distance of the pub. Why does that matter?"

"I wonder if he talks to God about his interest in the afterlife?"

Ruby started the motorcar. "I have a feeling I'll need my best hat and smart dress for tomorrow, won't I?"

"So shall I. We're going to church."

I rarely attended church. I had no quibbles with people who had a strong faith, but the horrors of the Great War had me questioning many things, my faith included. I was glad people sought comfort through church services and prayer, but it wasn't for me.

So, I was a trifle out of my depth as I stood at the back of St Giles's church next to Ruby during a midmorning service.

The church was a small, pleasant building, built over nine-hundred years ago, and subsequently demolished, rebuilt, and expanded over the years. A helpful information stand in the vestibule detailed the installation of stained-glass windows. It was a traditional layout with two rows of wooden pews set on either side of an aisle leading up to the podium and altar.

It was chilly inside the church, and I was glad I'd worn my warmer wool suit and a pair of fawn-coloured gloves. Ruby was extravagantly dressed in a striking cream outfit with a large hat and inappropriately high heels.

"I didn't think it would be so busy," she whispered as we sat after a rousing hymn.

"Reverend Worthington's jolly service must encourage the numbers." Some of the church services I'd attended as a child had been drier than a desert, and the most ardent worshippers had struggled to keep their eyes open.

"I like the hymns," Ruby said. "I remember these from school."

Reverend Worthington finished his sermon with a suitable passage from the Bible, then everyone slowly shuffled out of their pews, stopping now and again to chat with friends.

We waited, watching discreetly, to see if Mr Cloister was among the congregation. It had been impossible to make him out from only a back view, but there were several men who looked like him. We just needed to get a glimpse of faces, to be certain.

"There's Millicent!" Ruby whispered.

It took me a moment to spot her in the crowd of parishioners inching out of the pews. She was weaving across the aisle and into an opposite pew, heading towards one of the men who could be Mr Cloister.

I sucked in a breath. "That's Mr Cloister! They're meeting."

"I didn't know they were friendly," Ruby said.

"I'd be surprised if they were. After all, he'd be as interested in Millicent's great-grandmother as Mr Lombard. If there was a story to tell about her ghost, he'd tell it."

We stopped all pretense of picking up handbags and adjusting coats to watch their interaction.

Mr Cloister was stooped, listening intently to Millicent and occasionally shaking his head.

"Millicent is on the warpath again," Ruby said. "Perhaps she's gotten wind Mr Cloister is interested in her great-grandmother. He could be planning another ghost investigation at the Craven Arms."

"If that's his agenda, it's the first I've heard about it," I said. "And I won't allow it. The last one was too disturbing."

"Good for the dogs' home, though," Ruby said. "Think of the positive. More money for bedding and food."

I nodded absently. The conversation between Millicent and Mr Cloister had grown heated, and she stepped closer and jabbed a finger against his chest.

The church was almost empty, apart from a few slow-moving old ladies who required assistance to get down the outside steps, pausing to speak to Reverend Worthington, who stood by the exit.

"Let's go over," I said. "Find out what the problem is."

We wriggled out of the pew and dashed over.

"We had a deal," Millicent said.

"I promised you nothing." Mr Cloister looked up as we approached and straightened, adjusting his tie. "Good morning, ladies. I didn't know you came to this church."

Millicent turned around, and her cheeks flushed. "They don't. I've never seen either of them here before. What are you doing here?"

"Looking for answers," I said. "How about you?"

"This is my local church," Mr Cloister said. "I attend services as often as work will allow."

"I come when I'm in the area," Millicent said. "I'm usually busy on a Sunday, though."

"But you made a special effort because you knew I'd be here." There was a smug tinge to Mr Cloister's voice.

"I didn't realise you were friends," I said.

"We're most definitely not friends." Millicent tugged the hem of her jacket. "I need to go."

I blocked her path. "You were having a disagreement. I hope it wasn't about your great-grandmother."

"This has nothing to do with you," Millicent said. "Let me pass."

Mr Cloister smirked. "I'm happy to share the secret if she won't. I have nothing to hide."

"Keep quiet," Millicent snapped. "This is business. It has nothing to do with anyone else."

"What business are you involved in?" I asked.

Mr Cloister placed his hands behind his back and rocked on his heels. "For all Millicent's high and mighty behaviour about wanting to protect her great-grandmother's reputation, all she's interested in is getting a cut of the book profits."

Chapter 20

"I asked for no such thing!" Millicent had her hands on her hips, her cheeks flaming with indignation and possibly embarrassment at being caught out. "And unless you want me to cause a scene, let me pass so I can leave the church."

Mr Cloister continued to look smug. "Why would I lie? It would only be me out of pocket if I did a deal with you. Millicent knows Nicholas has signed me to be his leading expert in paranormal investigations, so she sought me out."

"You've secured a publishing deal with Nicholas?" I asked.

Mr Cloister lifted his chin. "We came to an acceptable arrangement. I'm finishing the mess William started and then working on my own series of books. I've got files of evidence I can use, so I should have my first book out early next year."

"Why would I be interested in your grubby little paranormal investigations?" Millicent asked.

"For the same reason, William interested you," Mr Cloister said. "You discovered a pot of gold and thought you were entitled to some of it. Afraid not, old girl."

"How did you learn of Mr Cloister's publishing deal?" Ruby asked Millicent.

"I don't know about any deal!" Millicent said. "Why do you care, anyway?"

"The Craven Arms is my concern. And it's where Mr Lombard died. I must ensure justice is done," I said.

"And write a story about it, no doubt," Mr Cloister said. "We're all here for the same reasons. Money and fame."

"There will be a suitable story published about the events at the pub," I said. "But that's not the reason we came to church today."

"I've had enough of this." Millicent attempted to barge past Ruby, but she planted her feet and held firm to prevent her from leaving.

"Let me go!" Millicent turned and shoved my shoulder. "Why do you believe him over me?"

"Mr Cloister has a valid point," I said. "Why would he lie?"

"She tried the same stunt with William and he turned her down, too," Mr Cloister said. "Millicent said if he intended to exploit her ancestors, she wanted money. Of course, he wouldn't agree. It would have opened a floodgate for any relatives of the deceased to come crawling with their hands out."

"She was my great-grandmother!" Millicent said. "I didn't want Mr Lombard writing about her because it was disrespectful."

"If he'd paid you, you wouldn't have given a hoot what he wrote," Mr Cloister said. "If the police hadn't arrested Grace for his murder, I'd say Millicent was mean enough to kill. Don't you agree, ladies?"

I glanced at Ruby. It was a thought. If what Mr Cloister said was true, Millicent could have been angry enough to get revenge. Mr Lombard was making money off her ancestor's exploits, and she got nothing.

Millicent tried another shove, still failing to get past. "I must go. I'm needed in early at work. I can't afford to lose my job."

"At the Savoy," Mr Cloister said. "Which is where Millicent overheard me doing business with Nicholas."

"Stop telling lies!" Millicent's raised voice echoed off the stone church walls.

"Is there something I can assist with?" Reverend Worthington appeared at the end of the pew, looking anxious.

"Help me. I'm being held against my will," Millicent said. "Mr Cloister is lying about me, and these nosy old bags think I'm guilty of murder."

"We never said you were guilty of anything," I said. "But it is curious you wanted money from Mr Lombard and then Mr Cloister. Would you have been happy for the ghost investigation to go ahead if you'd received payment?"

Millicent scowled fiercely. "I do what I must to get by. I've got no one to support me, and I'm not married."

"What a surprise," Mr Cloister murmured.

Millicent tried to stamp on his foot, but he leaped out of the way. "The wages aren't great at the Savoy. Not for those of us in the lower positions."

"To confirm, you did ask Mr Lombard for money?" I asked.

Millicent met my level stare with a ferocious glower. "Why not? He was rolling in the stuff. He'd published several books, and according to his publisher, the next one was pegged to be a bestseller."

"I thought Mr Lombard only mentioned your ancestor in passing?" I asked. "Why would you think he'd pay you for something so small?"

Mr Cloister cleared his throat. "We're expanding to an entire chapter on the infamous Annie and her highway robbery. Her fascinating criminal activities, followed by a gruesome death, and then her return as a ghost, are of interest to many. William was toying with the same idea, but he made the mistake of approaching Millicent to obtain more information. That must have been when she hit upon the idea to ask for a handout."

Millicent wheeled on Mr Cloister, making him jerk back in alarm. "Even if I asked for money, it didn't mean I killed Mr Lombard. It wasn't me."

"Perhaps everybody will feel calmer after tea and cake." Reverend Worthington fairly quivered with anxiety as his hallowed ground was smeared with anger. "We're serving in the hall next door. You're all welcome to join us. We can continue a calm conversation in a more comfortable setting. Sweet tea always settles the nerves."

"I'm not staying here to be accused of something I didn't do." Millicent hopped over the pew in a show of nimble agility. She sprinted to the end of the row and ran out of the church.

"Oh dear." Reverend Worthington's jaw trembled. "Millicent was always a headstrong young thing. I remember her visiting the church when she was a child. So full of passion. Although it seems to have slipped into anger."

Mr Cloister chuckled. "She'd be smiling if she'd gotten her hands on my money. Thanks for the offer of cake, Reverend, but I'll pass." He nodded at us and wandered out of the church.

I turned to Reverend Worthington. "My apologies for causing a scene. I was curious when I saw the argument. I fear our involvement only heated the situation."

"That's quite all right. I've been a vicar for almost twenty-five years, so I've seen plenty of action. I've served in several slum areas and even a parish in rural Kent."

"That sounds idyllic," Ruby said. "The rural parish, not the slums."

"You would think so, but some of the things village folk get up to would turn your hair white." Reverend Worthington gazed over our heads, a faraway look in his eyes, as if he was dredging memories. "People always think the cities are more dangerous, but I wonder if rural dwellers get bored living in the middle of nowhere with nothing to do, so their minds turn to dark deeds."

"I couldn't bear to live in the countryside," Ruby said. "All those strange animal noises in the middle of the night. It's bad enough going back to my parents' home. Some of the wildlife sound like they're killing each other."

"They most likely are. A small country residence would be tolerable," I said. "I can imagine my life as a lady squire, romping the fields with a pack of adopted dogs."

"That's why you'd do it," Ruby said with a smile. "You want a home for all the strays."

"There are worse things to desire," I said. "Although I would miss the bustle of city living. And the convenience. Everything is a walk or a short car journey away."

"London has a unique sense of purpose. It's a city brimming with life and opportunity," Reverend Worthington said. "Would you ladies like to accompany me to the hall? My church warden, Mrs Papworth, makes an excellent Victoria sponge cake. You'd be most welcome to a slice."

Ruby nodded eagerly, so we walked out of the church with Reverend Worthington and into the cool morning breeze. He led us around the side of the church to a new building with green double front doors.

"We were glad to add this hall to the church. It took years of fundraising, but we've been able to offer it for community events and Cub Scout meetings. And the Women's Institute uses it every Wednesday," Reverend Worthington said. "There's even talk of holding exercise classes, and the Home Guard are regular visitors, too. Of course, it doesn't have the church's charm, but it's practical and much warmer in the winter."

"It sounds like it's being put to good use," I said.

Reverend Worthington held open the door for us. "Are you planning on becoming regular churchgoers in this parish?"

"Sadly not," Ruby said, sounding sincere. "We're only in the area because of all the business at the Craven Arms."

"Oh! Of course. Such a tragedy. I heard the police have charged Grace Vilein with William's murder."

"They're on the verge of doing so," I said. "We have our concerns, though. Grace may be innocent."

Reverend Worthington's eyes widened as he led us to a trestle table lined with green cups and saucers, two efficient-looking ladies in flowered aprons standing at one end, serving people. "I know Grace. Her family live not far from the church. The police even asked me about her character after the tragic events at the pub."

"Do you think Grace is capable of murder?" I asked, ignoring the gasps from the serving ladies who were listening to our conversation.

Reverend Worthington clasped his hands in front of him. "I always think I know a person's character after spending time with them. But behind closed doors, people often think and do dreadful things. I try to guide those who are troubled, but my reach only stretches so far."

"You had concerns about Grace?" I accepted a cup of tea from one of the ladies.

"I was concerned for her soul. I try not to make assumptions, but she attended so many of William's ghost summonings. She even mentioned that she'd gone away with him to a house that was supposed to be haunted." Reverend Worthington pressed his lips together. "It seemed wrong, an unmarried woman going away for such a long time with a man. Perhaps that's me being old-fashioned, but the situation made me uneasy."

"We heard about that," I said. "Grace was seeking to make contact with a dead relative."

"Yes, her grandmother. I knew her, too. They weren't regular churchgoers, but they attended services now and again. Usually at Christmas and Easter. She was a big-hearted woman, with an even bigger voice and personality. And I could tell she adored Grace." Reverend Worthington paused to take his own cup of tea and receive a large slice of delicious-looking Victoria sponge cake. "I know she felt her loss deeply."

Ruby nudged me and grinned at the sight of the scrumptious cake. Two layers of sponge with icing dusted on the top, and a filling of jam and buttercream. We got our cake and followed Reverend Worthington.

"I prayed for Grace on many occasions," he said. "Now, it's come to this. I want to believe all souls can be saved. Perhaps I'm wrong."

"Reverend! Miss Spalding would like a word." A smartly dressed woman with a tight brown perm and horn-rimmed glasses beckoned to him.

"If you'll excuse me, ladies. Duty calls." Reverend Worthington nodded at us and hurried away.

We took a moment to enjoy the cake, which was as delicious as it looked.

"I thought we were onto something when we saw Millicent and Mr Cloister arguing," Ruby said.

"This new information gives her a motive," I said. "But Millicent seemed more embarrassed than worried when her extortion efforts were revealed."

"She was embarrassed because she got caught out," Ruby said. "She claimed she was at the Craven Arms to protect her great-grandmother's reputation, when all she wanted was money. It's rather sad."

"And Millicent does have a temper. Perhaps she let it get the better of her."

"I still favour Mr Cloister and Nicholas working in cahoots. They'll reap the rewards now Mr Lombard is dead."

"Mr Cloister certainly seemed self-satisfied with his new situation," I said. "But how do we prove their involvement?"

"Good morning, ladies." The woman who'd called Reverend Worthington away joined us. "Would you like another slice of cake? Mrs Papworth always makes too much. She's such a generous soul."

Ruby's plate was already empty, and she instantly agreed to another slice.

"I've not seen you here before. Are you the vicar's new lady?" She addressed the question to me.

"Oh! No, I don't know Reverend Worthington well," I said.

"There's no need to be coy. If you're courting, I'm happy for him. I never thought he'd recover after the last one left in such a flurry of scandal."

"Reverend Worthington's wife left him?" Ruby asked. "We didn't know."

"He was never married. And I'm not one for gossip, but it was the talk of the parish for some time." The woman smiled at me. "When I saw you, and how the vicar paid you special attention, I instantly thought you were his type. He likes a healthy, plain-faced woman. He's not one for fancy hair, heels, and makeup." She glanced at Ruby.

I held back a smile. "How flattering. But I can assure you—"

"They vicar and Diane were childhood sweethearts," the woman continued, as if I hadn't spoken. "Then she broke his heart when she went travelling for three years and got herself trapped overseas when the war broke out."

"That's a sad story," Ruby said.

"We thought it would have a happy ending. Diane came home after the war ended, and they reunited. Reverend Worthington was so happy. He wanted to marry her. We were even making plans, not that we said anything to the vicar. It would have been a delight to see him settled with a respectable lady." She glanced over her shoulder to make sure no one was listening. "Of course, then we discovered there was nothing respectable about her."

"Why would that be?" I asked.

"Diane ran off with a famous author and broke his heart all over again." She turned and waved at someone. "I must get on. If I leave the tea urn unattended for too long, it explodes. Enjoy your cake."

The cake was a lump in my stomach as I digested this news. We'd been wrong all this time.

Chapter 21

"Veronica, you're absolutely certain about this?" Inspector Templeton stood with me by the bar in the Craven Arms. It was only half an hour before lunchtime opening, so we needed to be quick.

"It all makes sense," I said. "And we've gone over everything several times. We've been looking at the wrong people for Mr Lombard's murder. All the suspects we identified are innocent."

"It's such a stroke of luck we went to church this morning," Ruby said. "Or we'd never have talked to the local gossip and discovered the shocking secret that solves this mystery."

Inspector Templeton rubbed his forehead. "It makes an uncomfortable kind of sense. But we'll need a confession. The evidence we have isn't enough to bring charges."

"But it's something. And it's enough to make a god-fearing man repent. We'll get you your confession." There was a knock at the main door of the pub. "That must be your police officers with the suspects."

Joe unlocked the main door and ushered in Inspector Templeton's men, along with Millicent, who looked furious at being dragged away from work. Mr Cloister and Nicholas entered next, both wearing an air of bored resignation. Grace scuttled in, looking terrified, and Reverend Worthington appeared, looking confused.

"I hope this won't take long," Nicholas said. "I'm missing valuable drinking time."

"We are in a pub," I said. "You can begin drinking as soon as the doors officially open."

He wrinkled his nose and glanced around. "This is not my kind of establishment."

"I'll be fortunate if I don't get fired," Millicent snapped. "Why did you have to send a copper to my place of work? It can't be that urgent."

"Solving William Lombard's murder is urgent," I said. "We finally know who killed him and why."

"Thank you, Veronica," Inspector Templeton said, stepping forward. "I appreciate you all taking the time out of your day to be here. I understand it's not ideal, so we won't keep you long. Although we have been holding Grace in regard to the murder, new information has come to light that suggests she is innocent."

Grace audibly gasped. "I keep telling you, I didn't do it."

"It seemed likely you were involved, though," I said. "The police discovered you were in debt, despite telling me you spent barely any of your wages. It's safe to assume you spent the money on Mr Lombard's ghost summoning services."

Grace lowered her head. "He was so helpful, and I needed to keep paying him so he'd keep me connected to my gran."

"More fool you," Nicholas said. "His business was fraudulent. He exploited lonely people with more money than sense."

"Steady on," Mr Cloister said. "Some of us are believers. If you speak out of turn in public, it'll damage my book sales."

"Oh, my public face always favours ghosts. But between us, there's no such thing. People have wild imaginations, little sense, and want to believe in the extraordinary. There's nothing of the sort out there."

A glass at the end of the bar fell to the floor and smashed, making us all jump.

"Are you sure there's no such thing as ghosts?" Mr Cloister asked. "It seems you've upset the spirits living here."

"Stuff and nonsense," Nicholas said. "Get on with it. Who killed William? We all thought it was Grace."

"Everyone at the ghost hunt had an opportunity to poison Mr Lombard." I jumped in before Inspector Templeton could draw a breath. "And while Grace gifted him an expensive bottle of red wine where the poison was hidden, the wine was uncorked and left to breathe behind the bar. It would have been a simple matter for anyone to drop the poison into the wine without being observed."

"Although Grace was always our prime suspect, it came to light that Nicholas had fallen out with Mr Lombard shortly before his murder," Inspector Templeton said. "Apparently, he was late in delivering the final chapters of his book, which meant the publication date needed to be pushed back."

Nicholas adjusted his tie. "Artistic types can never be relied upon. They blast past deadlines as if it's a proud achievement, when all it does is mess with my schedule, the printers, and the designers. It's inconvenient. But we're used to it. It's a hazard of the publishing industry. You don't see me killing other authors because they miss their deadlines. William was no different."

"You saw an opportunity to remove him and replace him with Mr Cloister," I said. "Perhaps the two of you were in on it together? It was clear during the ghost hunt that Mr Cloister was desperate to fill Mr Lombard's shoes. It would have been simple for you to act together that night—one causing a distraction, while the other slipped the poison into the wine."

"I had nothing to do with this." Mr Cloister's face paled. "I'll admit, I was envious of William and his notoriety. He had everything I wanted. But I was making a name for myself. It's just happening much faster now William is dead."

"Which is a great motive for you to kill him," Inspector Templeton said.

Mr Cloister shook his head and looked at Nicholas for support, but he only shrugged.

"And then we have Millicent. She was angry because Mr Lombard abused her ancestor's memory," I said. "But it turns out that's not the whole truth. Millicent wasn't concerned about her great-grandmother's legacy being besmirched. It was more that she felt entitled to a cut of the publishing profits when Mr Lombard's book was released."

"I've already told you why I did that." Millicent's tone was unapologetic. "It's hard to get by living in London on a server's wage."

"You're angry enough to commit murder," Mr Cloister said. "You bruised my shoulder when you shoved me in the church."

"You'll recover," Millicent snapped. "And go on to write more lies about other people's ancestors."

"If people buy the lies we produce, we'll keep publishing them," Nicholas said. "Just as you make no apologies for attempting to exploit an opportunity, neither do I."

Millicent huffed to herself. "I didn't kill Mr Lombard. Besides, I live ten stories up in a block of flats. I know strychnine was used, and I don't own any because I don't have a rat problem. They don't like the stairs. Too lazy to climb, I suppose."

"You could have bought some on the sly," Mr Cloister said, "to get rid of one large rat you had an issue with because he refused to fund your lifestyle."

Millicent scowled at him. "My lifestyle involves barely getting by. There's little to fund."

"Which gives you even more reason for going after William."

She rounded on Mr Cloister, her hands in fists. "Why would I kill him if I wanted his money?"

"Are you sure this isn't some mix-up?" Reverend Worthington asked. "I understand there are concerns about poison being found in William's body, but surely, the fall killed him?"

"He drank nearly an entire bottle of poisoned wine," Inspector Templeton said. "That dose was lethal. There would have been nothing a medical expert could have done to save him. The fall was caused because Mr Lombard felt unwell, due to the poisoning."

Reverend Worthington nodded, still looking uncertain.

"You all have credible motives for wanting Mr Lombard dead," I said. "But there was one motive and one clue that stood out from all the rest."

The group waited for me to continue. I looked at Inspector Templeton, and he nodded. I was almost surprised. He usually tutted and interfered, so I appreciated his confidence in me to see this through until the end.

"Reverend Worthington has been involved in this parish for many years and has gotten to know most of you through the church," I said. "Our encounters show him to be a generous, open-hearted man, always willing to share. Unfortunately, there was one thing he didn't want to share with anyone else. That one thing, or one person, was what Mr Lombard took from him."

All eyes swivelled to the vicar.

"I don't understand," Reverend Worthington said. "I had nothing to do with the death. I was at the Craven Arms to offer solace to anyone who became fearful when dabbling in matters that should best be left alone."

"We've been reliably informed that a lady you were particularly fond of fell in love with a famous author," I said. "Diane returned from overseas after the war, and you were hopeful you would marry. You must have introduced her to Mr Lombard when he was passing through on a book tour, or perhaps when he visited the parish to research his new book."

"I... I don't recall," Reverend Worthington stammered. "And I've already told the police I didn't know the man. He wasn't local to my parish."

"You lost Diane to Mr Lombard, though, didn't you?" I asked.

Reverend Worthington's nervy gaze went around the group. "I'm dedicated to the church. A passing fancy with a woman of no consequence means little to me."

"She wasn't a passing fancy, though," Inspector Templeton said. "After Veronica learned what happened to your relationship, we spoke to your parish warden and your sister. They confirmed Diane Madden lived next door to you when you were children growing up in the East End. When you joined the church, you remained in touch, and there was a continued affection between you."

"My personal life is none of your business," Reverend Worthington spluttered. "Yes, I've known Diane for many years, but she was a neighbour, nothing more."

"It must have been hard to keep a relationship going because you had to move wherever the Church sent you," I said. "But you never lost hope that you and Diane would one day marry. Then she went overseas, and that hope died. Especially when the war seemed endless."

"We all had struggles to endure during that difficult time," Reverend Worthington said.

"But then Diane came home," Inspector Templeton said. "We know she moved here. She sought you out. Your sister told us that she wanted a quiet life and to settle down."

"That must have made you happy," I said. "Finally, what you've always wanted was coming true."

Reverend Worthington frowned, his forehead glistening with sweat. "My sister shouldn't gossip. I've told her many times, it's not the behaviour of a godly woman."

"Then Mr Lombard came along with his flashy lifestyle, extravagant claims, and relative fame as an author," I said. "It's easy to see how Diane's head could have been turned. She thought she wanted a simple life as a vicar's wife, serving this parish, but she was presented with a chance to have a life as a famous author's wife. Travelling the country and potentially the world. There are few who could resist such a temptation."

"William never had a serious girlfriend." Nicholas's gaze was alight with curiosity. "He was always dating, but said he never wanted to settle because he was having too much fun with his fans."

"Diane wasn't to know that, though," Inspector Templeton said. "We tracked her down an hour ago and spoke to her at some length on the telephone. She was angry because Mr Lombard had lied to her. He claimed to be serious about the relationship and even professed an interest in marriage. It was a ruse. Once he got what he wanted from her, he stopped calling."

"Is Diane well?" Reverend Worthington's expression was creased with concern. "I don't have an address for her or a telephone number. I've been so concerned since she left."

"She's well enough, although she was shocked to learn of Mr Lombard's murder. Diane is moving to Spain," Inspector Templeton said. "After everything that happened here, she said she wanted a fresh start."

"Sadly, Diane will be even more shocked when she learns it was you who put the poison in the wine," I said to Reverend Worthington.

Several people in the assembled group gasped, although Nicholas looked thoroughly amused by the situation. He was probably wondering if he could get the vicar to sell his story and make money off of him.

"William wooed Diane with a lie," Reverend Worthington said after a long pause. "He duped her and told her that her dead father had spoken to him. He only said that to get her alone, so he could charm her. I confronted him and told him to stop bothering Diane."

"How did Mr Lombard respond?" I kept my tone level, despite my excitement lifting. We were about to hear the truth.

"He laughed at me. He thought it was a joke to play with people's emotions and exploit their weaknesses. It made me angry."

"So you killed him?" Millicent asked, a look of unmasked astonishment on her face.

"No! It wasn't me."

"It was you. And you would have gotten away with it," I said. "Nobody pays much attention to an amiable vicar moving through the crowd making polite conversation about the weather. It would have been easy for you to hide a dose of strychnine in a pocket and poison the wine."

"How did he know Willian would be at the Craven Arms?" Grace asked.

"Nicholas invited him," I said. "He told me at the investigation that he always invites local clergy to ghost events."

Nicholas nodded. "It helps to stop too many theatrics if a vicar is ambling about. I still can't figure out why you think it was him."

"Because Reverend Worthington made a mistake. Two, actually," I said.

Reverend Worthington stared at me, unblinking.

"When I first discovered Mr Lombard's body at the bottom of the cellar steps, there was a smell about him I couldn't identify."

"We thought it was connected to the poison used," Inspector Templeton said. "But when we discovered it was strychnine, we knew that couldn't be true."

"Unfortunately, I'm not privy to the full autopsy report, but I asked Inspector Templeton to have a thorough look at everything discovered on Mr Lombard's body," I said. "What do you think they found?"

"I couldn't tell you," Reverend Worthington said. "I'm no expert in matters such as that."

"A peppermint. The same brand of peppermints you're often seen popping into your mouth."

"How did one of the vicar's peppermints end up on the body?" Grace almost whispered.

"Reverend Worthington poisoned Mr Lombard, but when he heard his cries for help during the ghost hunt, he panicked. He thought if we got to Mr Lombard in time, he could be saved. So, in the dark, Reverend Worthington crept behind the bar, got the key to unlock the cellar door, and pushed Mr Lombard down the stairs. He was determined he wouldn't survive."

"And in your panic, you almost choked on your peppermint," Inspector Templeton said. "I've checked the statements, and several people said they heard a strange wheezing noise. That was you. You managed to cough up the peppermint stuck in your throat, and it fell down the cellar steps and landed on Mr Lombard's body."

"Which was the source of the smell," I said. "Reverend Worthington, you were heartbroken by Diane rejecting you time and again, and when Mr Lombard laughed at you, something snapped."

Reverend Worthington hung his head. When his gaze lifted, his eyes were full of resigned acceptance. "William was evil, and his obsession with ghosts was unnatural. He confessed to me that he believed none of it, but he was happy to take people's money and exploit them. I was prepared to tolerate his ghost fakery, but when he took away the one person I loved more than anything, I acted. And I'm glad I did. The world is a better place without William Lombard in it."

I let out a relieved sigh. We had the confession we needed.

Inspector Templeton stepped forward with his officers. "That's good enough. Take the vicar away."

Chapter 22

"I'm still in shock that a respectable pillar of the community was involved in something so grievous." My mother sat at her dressing table, dabbing perfume behind her ears.

"Reverend Worthington had us all fooled. If it wasn't for his peppermint obsession and his panic, he'd be a free man." I stared at her suspiciously. "What's going on?"

"Why does anything have to be going on?" My mother moved on to examining a small selection of lipsticks.

"When you said we were having dinner together, I assumed you'd make an effort and sit at the dining table. But you're dressed up and smelling sweet. Are you thinking we should dine out?"

"My heart couldn't stand leaving the house and going to a busy restaurant. But it does no harm to make an effort now and again." My mother peered at me in the mirror's reflection. "Have you brushed your hair today?"

I smoothed down my messy locks. "I stopped at the dogs' home for a couple of hours after work. I wanted to see if they'd had any interest in our latest foster."

As if on cue, the lame puppy wandered into the bedroom, his adorable tail wagging, always happy to see us.

"We may as well accept he's here to stay," my mother said. "Even though my allergies have been dreadful since he moved in, I like having his cheerful face around. And Matthew seems brighter since you brought him here."

"If the puppy is staying, he needs a name," I said.

"I've already thought of one." Matthew appeared in the doorway. Unusually for him, his clothes weren't crumpled, and he'd even shaved.

"What name have you chosen?" I asked.

"Felix. It's a good steady name. And he likes it."

"Are you sure you want the responsibility of a dog?" I asked. "You'll have no objections from me if you take him on, but he will require daily walks."

"I'll figure something out." Matthew looked away. "And the garden is big. I know the neighbours will help, too."

"Matthew, that won't be enough for a growing dog. Only take him on if you feel you're up to it. Remember, dogs can live for over a decade."

He shrugged. "It's not as if I've got anything else to do."

"You'll find work eventually," I said. "Something good is just around the corner."

There was a knock at the front door.

"Matthew, answer that," my mother said. "We can't leave our guests outside for long."

"We have guests for dinner?" I crouched and stroked the puppy.

"Given how hard you've been working, I decided you needed a treat." Her gaze lit with amusement and she smiled. "Remember to be polite."

My eyes narrowed. "What have you done?"

Ruby appeared in the doorway, grinning.

"Oh! Ruby is always welcome at dinner," I said. "Especially since she's yet to move out."

"I'm tempted to stay forever," Ruby said. "I've been wonderfully spoiled. Veronica! You could have made an effort. Edith, you look marvellous." She kissed my mother's cheek.

"As do you, my dear. I wish your flair for fashion would rub off on my daughter."

"My outfit is perfectly decent to have dinner with the family," I said.

Ruby's eyes widened. "You haven't told her, have you?"

My mother fussed with her pearls. "I wanted it to be a surprise."

"Will someone tell me what's going on?" I scowled at Ruby, but she simply tittered into her hand.

Inspector Templeton arrived in the doorway, looking dapper in a smart suit, his hair slicked back and his chin freshly shaven. "Good evening, Veronica."

"What are you doing here?" I asked.

"That's no way to greet our guest." My mother stood and accepted kisses on both cheeks from Inspector Templeton. "I know you've both been working jolly hard on making sure Ruby's poisoner was discovered. That deserves a special dinner. Matthew cooked a chicken pie with all the trimmings. And there's a trifle for dessert.

Is that wine for the table?" She gestured at the bottle of red wine in Inspector Templeton's hand.

"It is." He passed it over.

"It had better not be poisoned," I muttered.

My mother swatted my arm as she left her bedroom. "We'll have aperitifs to start."

"Since when do we have aperitifs before dinner?" I whispered to Matthew.

He shrugged again. "Mother wants to make a good impression."

"Why? Does she want to marry Inspector Templeton?"

He chuckled as he picked Felix up. "No, but I have a feeling she wants you to."

"Good grief! This is her attempt at matchmaking?"

"You could pick a worse fellow. He's always watching out for you and Ruby."

"Inspector Templeton tells us off and repeatedly threatens to put us behind bars for interfering in police matters."

"You need someone who'll make sure you don't get too big for your boots. You always were headstrong, even when we were growing up."

"I'm confident. There's a difference." I suddenly felt underdressed and wished I had done something to my hair. "You should have told me he was visiting."

"It's not like Inspector Templeton hasn't had dinner with us before. Come on. I made a real effort with the pie."

I was torn between mortification and annoyance as I followed my family and Ruby into the dining room. I suppressed a groan. Mother had put out the best china and silverware, and Inspector Templeton was currently pouring wine into crystal glasses.

Ruby sidled over and nudged me with an elbow. "Don't be angry. Edith got in touch and said she wanted to surprise you."

"You're involved in this charade, too?"

"I twisted Inspector Templeton's arm to come. Although it didn't take much twisting. After everything we've been through, I got the impression he needed a relaxing evening with friends."

"He does appear tired," I said.

"Now the murder investigation is wrapped up, and Reverend Worthington has been charged, Inspector Templeton is being forced to focus on the slum clearances," Ruby whispered. "When we spoke, he downplayed it, but I could tell he was unhappy. He mentioned having to displace a number of homeless men."

"Removing them from the slum areas doesn't get rid of the problem. It just shifts it to another spot," I said.

"Oh, let's have fun this evening." Ruby laced her hand through my crooked elbow. "No serious talk about murder or society's problems. Life can be difficult, but we can have fun, too. When you and Jacob aren't sniping at each other, you get along famously."

"I'll put up with him being here," I said. "But I'm having words with my mother after this evening is over. I don't need her interfering in my personal life."

"That's what mothers do. The ones that care, anyway," Ruby said. "I adore my parents, but I can't remember the last time they asked about what I was getting up to. They focus only on the successful children."

I put an arm around my best friend's shoulders and squeezed tight. "I'll be sure to ask you lots of questions this evening. Especially if it keeps the heat off of me." I collected the puppy from Matthew and dumped him in Inspector Templeton's lap the second he sat in an armchair. "Be useful, Jacob, and take Felix for a walk."

Inspector Templeton stared at the dog. "Is this yours?"

"Matthew is considering adopting him. Puppies don't have the best bladder control, so it's best he's settled before we sit down to eat."

Inspector Templeton reared back as if fearing the puppy would commence toileting activities on his best suit.

I smiled benignly. "Once you're done, I want to talk about the Policeman's Ball."

Inspector Templeton gently placed the puppy on the floor. "What about it?"

"Every year, they give a percentage of proceeds to charity. This year, you should nominate the dogs' home."

"That's a splendid idea." Ruby joined us and handed around glasses of wine.

"If I do, does that mean I have to take you as my date?" Inspector Templeton asked, a wicked twinkle in his dark eyes.

My cheeks flushed. "If you must. But it'll be a business arrangement. I'll be the dogs' home representative."

"I must come too," Ruby said. "I'm sure you have a suitable single police officer in need of a date."

"I'm no matchmaker." Alarm flickered in Inspector Templeton's eyes.

"You're a capable man. I'm sure you can rustle up someone suitable for Ruby," I said.

He sat back in the seat and regarded me levelly, not breaking eye contact for such a long time that I grew flustered. "Let me see what I can do."

It had been almost a month since I'd cajoled Inspector Templeton into supporting the dogs' home through the Policeman's Ball. The charity was delighted to receive their support, and everything was arranged.

All I was waiting for was for Ruby to arrive, and our dates to collect us.

I checked my reflection and smoothed a stray strand of blonde hair off my face. I had made an effort and was wearing a pretty high-waisted cream dress with a beaded hem. I'd also had my hair styled, and was wearing a touch of makeup. After all, it wouldn't do to let down the dogs' home, and it was a black-tie event, so I didn't want to stand out for the wrong reasons.

And, I must admit, I felt a flicker of excitement about going as Inspector Templeton's date. It wasn't an official date, and I'd been clear that this was a business arrangement, but we would have a lovely evening. When Inspector Templeton wasn't being stern, he was excellent company. Maybe we'd even dance. There used to be wonderful dances at the local hall during the war. It was a great opportunity for people to let off steam and forget their troubles for an evening.

Not only would there be dancing, but we were being treated to a three-course dinner. There was also a raffle and an auction to raise money. It would be a thrilling evening.

I checked the contents of my small beaded handbag once more. I had everything I needed.

I slipped on my heels, which I'd worn around the house all week to break them in, and walked into my bedroom with Benji. Sadly, he wouldn't be coming to the ball, so he'd be keeping my mother, Matthew, and Felix—who was now an official member of the family—entertained for the evening.

"You look lovely." My mother was tucked under her sheets, a book open, and her glasses perched on the end of her nose. "Jacob will be bowled over when he sees you."

"This isn't for him." I did a little twirl in front of her to show off the dress.

"There's no harm in looking nice for your young man," she said.

I sighed. No matter how many times I told her, my mother would never accept that Inspector Templeton was just a friend. Sometimes, he wasn't even that.

"What time is Ruby getting here?" she asked. "I'm excited to see what extravagant dress she's wearing."

"She was due to arrive ten minutes ago," I said. "You know how dreadful her timekeeping is, so I deliberately told her an earlier time than necessary. Jacob and Ruby's date should arrive shortly."

"Be nice to Jacob this evening," my mother said. "I'm certain he's lonely. He works hard and then goes home to an empty house. It's nice you're keeping him company."

"He manages perfectly well," I said. "And I've told him to get a dog as a companion numerous times, but he won't listen to me."

"Sometimes, a person needs more than a dog as a companion," my mother said. "Nothing can replace the love of a good man. I still miss your father every day."

I perched on the edge of the bed and squeezed her hand. "So do I. I understand what you're saying, but I'm content. I have no need for anyone else in my life."

"Perhaps tonight will change your mind. Good food, music, dancing, and fun. Let down your barriers and let a good man in."

"I have the best man already." I patted Benji's soft head.

My mother sighed. "I don't know why I bother with you, child."

"Because you adore me, and you want the best for me." I kissed her cheek. "Matthew is around if you need anything. And don't wait up. I'll be back late."

"I won't be able to sleep while you're out. And the second you return, I'll insist on hearing your news."

I softly sighed. "I'll look in on you and see if you're awake when I return."

A loud thudding on the front door made me jump. "That must be Ruby. Goodness, she sounds desperate to get in. Maybe she needs to use our convenience before the gentlemen arrive."

"Hurry! And bring her in here so I can see her dress," my mother said. "Mark my words, she'll be in something flamboyant."

I dashed to the door and opened it. Ruby fairly fell through, her hand raised to thump on the door again.

"You're not late! Jacob and your date haven't arrived yet," I said.

Ruby grabbed my hands and stared at me. She opened her mouth, but nothing came out.

I winced at the tightness of her grip. "Is something wrong? You didn't have an accident on your way here, did you?"

"No!" Ruby gasped in a breath. "Veronica, it's terrible news. I couldn't believe it when I heard."

"Has the Policeman's Ball been cancelled?" Ruby's face was pale beneath her makeup, and there were tears in her eyes. "You're scaring me. Tell me what happened."

She swallowed loudly. "Jacob won't be coming tonight."

I squashed my disappointment. "He doesn't want me to accompany him?"

"It's not that. I took a telephone call from a friend who works on the exchange network. She knew I was going to the Policeman's Ball with you, and was worried we might be affected."

"Affected by what?" Ruby's panic was impacting on me and my stomach churned.

A tear trickled down Ruby's cheek. "There's been an explosion in a slum area the police have been clearing. Inspector Templeton, Jacob, was inside a building when the roof caved in. There's ... there's nothing left."

I grew lightheaded and struggled to breathe. "An explosion?"

Ruby threw her arms around me. "Veronica, they haven't been able to find him."

Historical notes

London's pubs are steeped in history, and some are rumoured to be haunted by restless spirits, so I had to include a mystery featuring a ghostly suspect. I could have researched this topic for months, since there are so many fascinating stories to enjoy.

In 1920s London, there was a growing interest in the supernatural, particularly psychic phenomena. This included a fascination with ghosts and communication with the dead.

Organisations such as the Society for Psychical Research (founded in 1882) investigated claims of the paranormal. However, their focus was more scientific and academic than the ghost hunts of today. There were also individual figures like Harry Price, who emerged in the 1920s and 30s, investigating hauntings and promoting public interest in the paranormal.

Here are some tales of ghostly patrons that inspired me to send Veronica, Ruby, and Benji on a haunted ghost tour:

The Ten Bells, Spitalfields: This pub has a particularly grim connection to Jack the Ripper. One of his victims, Annie Chapman, was last seen alive drinking here in 1888. Her ghost is said to haunt the pub, with patrons reporting disembodied moans and cold spots.

The Prospect of Whitby, Wapping: This riverside pub dates back to the 1500s and has a long and colourful history. A down-on-his-luck sailor is said to have wandered into the pub and never left. Patrons have reported sightings of a man in a tattered peacoat, with some feeling a cold hand on their shoulder! There's also a rumour a mean-spirited judge roams the building and people have seen ghostly pirates who were hung nearby.

The Grenadier, Belgrave Square: This former officer's mess has a soldier who won't leave. He was killed after he failed to pay a gambling debt. The pub is covered in dollar bills, with tourists and ghost hunters helping the soldier pay off his debt. Customers report a chill in the air, while staff have reported a presence in the cellar, footsteps, and sighs.

The Spaniards Inn, Hampstead: Built in 1585 as a toll gate, it's rumoured the inn got its name from two Spanish landlords and brothers, who fell in love with the same woman, fighting a duel to win her hand. One brother was killed and now haunts the pub. Another ghost, Dick Turpin, is also said to enjoy his afterlife here. The highwayman was allegedly born here and hid his loot in the pub. Customers hear neighing and hooves in the carpark from his famous horse, Black Bess.

The Volunteer, Marylebone: Only a few doors down from 221B Baker Street (Sherlock Holmes), the pub is named after it served as a recruiting station during the Second World War. Prior to that, it was a private house, owned by Rupert Neville and his wealthy family. However, in 1654, a fire destroyed the mansion, killing everyone inside. Only the cellars survived, and that is where Rupert Neville's ghost lives. He's been seen in the bar and his ghostly footsteps have been heard.

Also by

Death at the Fireside Inn
Death at the Drunken Duck
Death that the Craven Arms
Death at the Dripping Tap

More mysteries coming soon. While you wait, why not investigate the back catalogue of K.E. O'Connor (Kitty's alter ego.)

About the author

Immerse yourself into Kitty Kildare's cleverly woven historical British mysteries. Follow the mystery in the Veronica Vale Investigates series and enjoy the dazzle and delights of 1920s England. Kitty is a not-so-secret pen name of established cozy mystery author K.E. O'Connor, who decided she wanted to time travel rather than cast spells! Enjoy the twists and turns.
Join in the fun and get Kitty's newsletter (and secret wartime files about our sleuthing ladies!)

Newsletter: https://BookHip.com/JJPKDLB
Website: www.kittykildare.com
Facebook: www.facebook.com/kittykildare

Printed in Great Britain
by Amazon